Kira's Crossing

Orysia Davydiak

The Acorn Press
Charlottetown
2020

ACØRNPRESS

P.O. Box 22024
Charlottetown, Prince Edward Island
C1A 9J2
acornpresscanada.com

Printed in Canada
Edited by Penelope Jackson
Designed by Matt Reid

Library and Archives Canada Cataloguing in Publication

Title: Kira's crossing / Orysia Dawydiak.
Names: Dawydiak, Orysia, 1952- author.
Identifiers: Canadiana (print) 2020021327X | Canadiana (ebook) 20200213288 |
ISBN 9781773660585 (hardcover) | ISBN 9781773660592 (HTML)
Classification: LCC PS8607.A968 K54 2020 | DDC jC813/.6—dc23

The publisher acknowledges the support of the
Government of Canada, the Canada Council for the Arts,
and the Province of Prince Edward Island.

To all the people who work tirelessly for
the health and conservation of our oceans and
of the lakes and rivers that feed them.

Dear Beth ~
Some 'light' summer
reading for you!
Love,
Orysia

Contents

Chapter 1: The Pendright...............................1

Chapter 2: Merrowmind Council.............................13

Chapter 3: Janus......................................22

Chapter 4: Reconnaissance 28

Chapter 5: Strange Alliance...............................38

Chapter 6: Merrows in Arms......................................53

Chapter 7: Operation Free Merhaven......................66

Chapter 8: After Freedom 75

Chapter 9: Crystal Clear.................................82

Chapter 10: Showtime................................92

Chapter 11: A Favour Repaid............................... 102

Chapter 12: Sea to Sea.................................. 111

Chapter 13: The Laboratory 122

Chapter 14: Merrow Gardens............................... 134

Chapter 15: In the Name of Science 141

Chapter 16: Dr. Giles Morton 147

Chapter 17: Old Nemesis................................. 156

Chapter 18: Sea Lion Cove.................................. 165

Chapter 19: Finding Home 177

Chapter 1 –
The Pendright

KIRA CONSIDERED THE HARBOUR BELOW, shimmering under the warm June sun. Only a week since high school graduation, but her disappointment had not abated. That was behind her now, and she needed to focus on what lay ahead: her summer job at Jimmy's Caprine Creamery and her departure for university in the fall. She'd narrowed down her choices to two schools, the University of British Columbia on the West Coast and Memorial University on the East. Both offered excellent marine biology programs, but Memorial was much closer to home. Cody had chosen UBC out West, four time zones away.

Cody, her best friend and kindred spirit, had not come home for the ceremony, had not been there to share the celebration with her. She'd found herself on the outside as usual, watching her classmates' revelries, withdrawing as she had before she befriended Cody. Maybe not such an outsider anymore, Kira thought. She'd grown a thicker skin, and she had her mermaid scales to protect her now. Her family had expanded to include an entire merrow and merrow-friendly community living on her eastern shore.

Nope, Cody smarty-pants had zoomed past her and all their classmates, starting university a year ahead of everyone else. He was brilliant. He had aced the marine technology entrance exams, so it would have been foolish not to accept the scholarship and go. The entire community was proud of him, the first person from their tiny fishing village to attend university.

Kira knew she should be happy for him, and she was. However, an emptiness, like constant hunger pangs, would not leave her—no matter that she had two sets of parents who adored her: Cillian and Bess Cox, her adoptive parents, as well as Currin and Calista, her rescued biological parents. Because she'd only known them for the past five years, she thought of Currin and Calista more as an uncle and aunt. That made sense, since her cousins Borin and Amelie lived with them. She had come to adore Amelie after a rocky first encounter with her cousins, and her younger cousin reciprocated those feelings. But Borin, who was Kira's age, kept his distance and remained cool toward her. She had no other close friends, no one who could replace Cody, her first true friend and confidant.

She considered running down to the rocky beach below and throwing herself into the ocean. Normally that would cheer her up, sliding along the bottom, peeking through the seaweed forest for starfish, crabs, and sea urchins. She could zip past schools of fish, maybe join a small herd of playful seals chasing each other, leaping out of and into the surf.

Kira glanced at her watch and sighed. It was time for her shift at the creamery. She walked back into the house to change into her green uniform with a pair of frolicking white goats on the front and white letters on the back that read *No kidding! Eat chèvre*. At first, most of the villagers didn't know that *chèvre* meant "goat cheese" in French. Kira had been learning French and Spanish in school and was proud to introduce new terms when she could. Jimmy was happy to accommodate her. He was her next best friend and always ready to listen to her and offer words of encouragement or sympathy or whatever she needed. When she arrived at the creamery, she was disappointed to learn that Jimmy was up at the farm.

Ginny grinned at Kira's woeful expression. "Cheer up, dearie. Jimmy was in goat withdrawal. He's been so glum the last couple of days, had to get his goat fix. No one likes a mopey boss." She laughed while wrapping up bricks of cheddar goat cheese on the side counter. Ginny was another landed merrow, about her mother Bess's age, and always quick to find humour in any situation.

Kira stepped up to the cash register and pulled out the account book and a calculator. She tried to concentrate on the math, pushing aside her compounded disappointments. "Looks like we had a busy day," she finally said.

"Yes," Ginny replied. "There should be enough cheese in the front case for tomorrow and the next day. The brie won't be ready until Friday."

"Okay, I'll start the current inventory now if you can stay here in the front. That'll keep me busy for two hours anyway." Kira closed the sales account book and pulled out a large binder from behind the counter.

"Sure. Are you already bored this early in the summer?" Ginny smiled at Kira. "Heard anything from Cody lately?"

"No," Kira said. "Last time we talked was the day before graduation. He was way up near Alaska on the research ship. The line was terrible. I only heard a few words. I guess he was sorry he couldn't make it back home. He's been out there for two whole months, having a great time of course." She pouted.

Ginny raised her eyebrows, and her eyes sparkled. "Oh? You think he found a girlfriend? That kind of fun?"

"No!" Kira snorted and then blushed. "I mean, he's such a science geek. He doesn't seem to notice girls. Only high tech on Cody's radar."

Ginny shook her head. "I don't know many eighteen-year-old boys who aren't interested in the opposite sex. But I know what you mean about Cody, Mr. One-Track Mind. Paid no attention to all the girls drooling over him last summer before he left. Cody's a good-looking young man now his braces are off and he's all grown up."

One of those smitten girls was Ginny's niece Glenda. Kira still had a hard time thinking of Cody as grown-up, but there was no doubt he had slimmed down and elongated like a poplar sapling. Long gone was the chubby boy who had introduced her to the wonders of tide pools five years ago. He was the first person who had seen her transform into a mermaid, and he had faithfully kept her secret.

They had shared their fascination with the underwater world for so long, it felt as if they had grown up together, like brother and sister. Each of them was the only child in their families. Kira had been aware of their physical changes as they matured into young adults, but their relationship never faltered. Now she felt uneasy about their separation on two sides of the continent, on two different oceans. Still, she believed that being in or near the sea was the one constant that would always keep them connected.

Kira shrugged and headed for the temperature-controlled rooms where the huge ripe cheese rounds were stored. "Cody's the youngest person aboard that ship," she said. "The rest are ancient, over thirty years old."

"Ha! Wait till you're thirty, young lady. See how ancient you feel then." Ginny's tinkling laughter followed Kira as she retreated through the swinging doors.

At the end of her shift, Kira did not return home directly. She'd been invited to have dinner with her royal merrow parents and her cousins who lived with them. She sensed something was up; Currin and Calista had been acting unusually cheerful of late. They were generally optimistic about life, but this was different. Kira couldn't imagine why they seemed to be extra happy, but she expected she would soon find out.

Her merrow parents had managed to adapt well to life in the small coastal village, just as they had on Hildaland. Of course, they were much more content once they were free and off that horrid prison island. Calista's skill as a weaver lent itself to filling a niche in the village. She opened a fibre shop in her home that sold locally spun yarns and handwoven items. She also taught and hired other newly landed merrows to knit for her shop. Her unusual patterns and use of colours soon attracted attention outside the village, and the business outgrew the space she had. With the help of carpenters, Currin built a large addition to their house with a separate entrance for the shop. Calista bought a second loom and hired an experienced weaver from a nearby village to keep up with the demand.

Meanwhile, Currin and Rik Bates, another landed merrow, began a small company that processed fish and shellfish at the far end of the village, close to the water. Their smoked herring and eels were so popular that they also had to hire extra help to keep up. They had considered expanding but were waiting to hear if the narrow road to their village would be widened and repaved by the local county government. The refrigerated trucks that could handle larger shipments were too wide for the current track that connected them to the nearest highway.

"Kira, come on in. Supper is almost ready." Currin greeted her at the door with a quick hug.

Kira always looked up at the round entranceway when she walked into their house. They had designed it themselves, so it stood out amongst all the rectangular and square clapboard houses in the village. The curves inside the house and the pearly white stucco on the exterior reminded Kira of Merhaven, the ancient merrow palace under the sea, now occupied by their enemies, the finfolk.

This terrestrial home of the king and queen of the Atlantic merrows was both a happy and a sad place for Kira. She was pleased they had been freed, but she knew they were devastated by the loss of their ancestral home. They seemed so content with life in the village that she was always afraid to mention anything that related to their former home beneath the sea.

When Kira appraised her merrow father, she thought of a great golden bear. He used his large, calloused hands, like powerful paws, to carve out his new life on land. He kept his fair strands of whorled hair long, as was the custom for merrows in their natural environment. At work, he tied it back. Most landed merrows preferred to cut it short like the native villagers. Currin didn't seem to mind the teasing, being called a hippie or bohemian or even Goldilocks. He was proud to be a merrow, though he realized that this was a topic never to be discussed with humans he didn't know well. Few people, even along the coast, knew that merrows existed, let alone that they lived among them. Except for certain features such as slightly larger eyes and hands, merrows on land were indistinguishable from land-based humans.

Amelie ran to Kira, her hands waving in the air. "Kira, you have to see what I made at art camp last week!" She grabbed Kira's arm and led her into the living room. On the mantle over the fireplace was a sparkling sculpture with eight frozen tentacles emerging from a dome in the middle. "Watch this!" Amelie plugged in a power cord. The dome lit up in green, faded to yellow, and then changed to pink, blue, purple, and red, pulsing with the changing colours.

Kira stepped closer and smiled. "It's Sherman, isn't it?"

"Yes, it is!" Amelie clapped her hands together. "I know it's not a perfect octopus. It's just an art project," she said, her tone apologetic.

"Oh no, it's amazing, Amelie. You are so talented. And you figured out how to wire it and use all the colours. I could never do that."

"Well, Borin helped with the wiring. But I designed it."

Calista walked in and greeted Kira with a hug and kiss. She then

6

crossed the room and put her arm around the black-haired, dark-eyed girl. The contrast between the aunt and niece was marked; the older woman, tall and slender with long honey-coloured hair, was a head taller than the solid, angular sixteen-year-old. Kira found Amelie striking in appearance, attractive if not delicate. Amelie's resemblance to her finfolk mother, Shree, had unnerved Kira when she first met her five years ago. But as she grew, her father Nim's softer features became more apparent. Nor did Amelie have a mean streak in her body, so Kira was hopeful that the merrow side of her ancestry would always prevail.

"She's gifted, this one," Calista said and squeezed Amelie's shoulders. The girl looked up at her aunt, beaming. Not that long ago, Kira would have felt slighted and even a little jealous to see her natural mother so close to her cousin. But she had accepted that no matter how evil Shree might be, she could not judge her cousins by their parents. Anyway, after Amelie and Borin had been separated from their parents, Kira's own birth parents had chosen to care for them. Just as Bess and Cillian Cox had adopted Kira when she was a year old after her parents had been captured and imprisoned.

"Okay, girls, dinner is ready. Amelie, will you get your brother, please?" Calista said and returned to the kitchen.

Amelie shook her head and muttered, "Yeah, if he'll leave the latest thing he's torn apart." Kira grinned at her cousin. Borin was as mechanically minded as Amelie was drawn to art. They both loved to work with their hands. They were clever at whatever they put their minds to. Like Kira, Borin had just graduated and was planning to leave for a community college in a nearby town. Unlike his sister, Borin was often cynical and given to brooding. His brow was perpetually creased, as if he were working out the solution for an intricate puzzle. More likely he was trying to piece together a disassembled motor.

Kira and Amelie were sitting at the table when Borin walked into the dining area. He looked down at Kira and slipped into his chair. "Hey," he mumbled. Currin gave him a disapproving frown.

"Hey yourself, mechano man," Kira said and shook her head slightly at Currin. "Are you in destructo or rebuilding mode right now?"

"You wouldn't think it was so funny if you knew what I was building," Borin grumbled. "Just one clue, it's for the kitchen. Something to help Calista." He looked up at his aunt, who was setting down a steaming bowl of greens in front of him. "Awesome! Sea greens *delectibus.*" When Currin added a large platter of fresh, pale grey mackerel fillets to the table, Borin pumped his right arm up and down. "All right!"

A proper merrow meal, Kira noted. Underwater, merrows would eat the fish whole—scales, heads, fins and all if they were small enough. Kira was happy to ingest both human and merrow food since she'd lived on land most of her life. There were species she would not eat—octopuses and seahorses, for instance: the first because they were so intelligent, and she considered them friends and allies; the second because they were too cute.

"So, Kira, the last time we spoke you were trying to decide between two schools. One on the West Coast, one on the East," Currin said between fishy mouthfuls. "Have you picked one yet?"

Before she could answer, Borin said, "Not just any school, Currin. An institution of higher learning."

Currin shot him a dark look, but Kira said, "No, I haven't picked one yet. I'm still looking at different universities."

"Why don't you go to the same college as Borin?" Amelie suggested. "You could get a ride together every day, and it would save a lot of money."

Borin's breath exploded. "Pah! There's nothing for her there. She's not a techie like me." He glared at his wide-eyed sister. "She has more important work to do. She's a true princess, remember? We're the half-breeds."

"Borin!" Currin protested. "None of that is relevant. Kira is free to make her own choices, just as you are."

"Well, it's true," he continued. "And if she were a merrow leader with a spine, interested in doing good for her kind, she'd be paying more attention to what's happening at Merhaven. Not making stupid goat cheese, or studying marine botany nonsense to help feed the world. Screw humans. What have they done for us? Polluted the oceans, killed most of the fish, destroyed the sea floor. That's what!" He pushed back his chair, arms up in the air in answer to Currin and Calista's objections. "I'm going back into my cave," he said, retreating to his room. "To work for my family."

Kira sat quietly, stunned at the outburst. Amelie sniffled, her eyes frightened, and looked to Calista for reassurance. Kira wondered which family Borin was referring to—Shree and Nim, who presumably still ruled over Merhaven, or his aunt and uncle, who had been raising him and his sister for the past five years? She'd always had reservations about his true allegiance. It didn't help that he continued to resent her all this time. Amelie, on the other hand, was forever the peacemaker.

Currin reached over to pat Kira's hand. "Never mind Borin. You know he gets easily frustrated. It was hard for him to accept his mother's—"

"Currin!" Calista interrupted, her arm around Amelie's shoulders, the girl's face stricken and tear streaked. "Come help me with dessert, Amelie, dear," she said and led her niece into the kitchen.

"I must say, that outburst was a surprise," Currin said with a grimace. "I had hoped we could have a nice meal to celebrate this occasion. Borin has fit in so well. I forget that he has not fully come to terms with the truth of his birthright."

Kira looked down at her plate. "I know, and here I am, a constant reminder of who he is not."

"That would apply equally to your mother and me."

"No, I was the one who showed up and turned his life upside down. He'll always blame me, deep inside, even if he knows it's not my fault that his mother is a fin—" Kira stopped herself from uttering the word in case Amelie might overhear. She whispered, "Maybe I should leave home sooner. I could find a job in St. John's or Vancouver. I have acceptances from both schools. I—"

"Stop, Kira. You cannot escape who you are, wherever you go. Borin will deal with this eventually. He needs to mature. It takes longer for us males to grow up." He gave Kira a wry smile. "Perhaps Borin has a point, though. Perhaps if you made some time for our Merrowmind Council, for instance, contributed to our plans for the future. I know you did not ask to be born to the royal line, but that is your reality. As it is Calista's and mine that we will never be able to take our merrow forms again."

At these words, Kira felt herself tearing up. She knew how frustrating it had been for him to accept that fact, once they were freed from Hildaland and he had the opportunity to test himself in the water. Kira would never forget the broken look on his face as he waded into the water and then back out in his now immutable human form. There was no going back for him, or Calista, or most of the previously captive merrows.

After the age of twenty-five or so, merrows who remained on land could no longer take on their merrow forms in the sea. And if they stayed underwater, they could not transform into humans on land. The youngest ones had been able to transform back and forth, all of them under twenty-five years of age. Those slightly older could sometimes regain their merrow morphology, but then they could not change back into human form. For several merrows, it was a tragic discovery. They had married humans while on Hildaland, and now they could no longer live together as a family. None of the mixed couples had children, so at least there were no young ones who lost a parent to the sea.

"Kira, you've seen much of our two worlds and are experienced enough to join us. Will you consider it? Even though you will be leaving, we would be honoured to include you in our council."

Calista walked in as Currin spoke the last words. Her sad eyes implored Kira to accept the invitation. Kira nodded, though uncertain how she could contribute to the council. Currin patted her hand.

"And now, the reason we asked you here today," he continued. "We have a royal heirloom that rightfully belongs to you."

Calista handed a small round white box to Currin.

"This may be the first time in merrow history that this Pendright will be worn by a female of our kind. Humans have crowns and scep-tres. We are more practical," Currin said as he opened the box and lifted out a glittering pendant.

He stood up, moving away from the table, and motioned for Kira to approach. She walked forward slowly, her legs trembling, her eyes mesmerized by the brilliant symbol of leadership and power. Two silvery spikes attached to a gold chain protruded in a V-shape from the top of a rounded half-dome. Overlapping iridescent pink and purple scales covered it. From the bottom, several gold spikes of varying lengths shot out, as if the entire pendant were a rocket blasting off.

Without realizing what she was doing, Kira kneeled before her royal parents while Currin began to chant. At first, she did not un-derstand his words, if that's what they were. Then he slowed down, opening up the chain and lifting it over her head. "Kira Corinalis of Atlanta Maris, sovereign princess of Oceana, you are hereby the rightful bearer of this Pendright. You are owed allegiance by all true merrows in your waters, as you owe protection to them. Remember the responsibility you are accepting, and your right to expect loyalty from your subjects."

Currin lowered the opened chain and Pendright over Kira's head until it rested around her neck. At the first contact with her skin, she felt an electric charge that made her gasp. A momentary burning sensation had Kira looking down to see if the Pendright was glowing. It sparkled for a second. Then the colours became subdued.

"Wow," she managed to say.

"On land, you may want to wear it under your clothes," Calista suggested. "And you'll find when you go into the sea, the Pendright will attach to your chest scales. It's quite stunning underwater but not visible to human eyes."

"Oh. Should I wear it just for special occasions?"

"No, dear, you're expected to wear it all the time. That's how you will be recognized as the royal sovereign."

Kira let out a small sigh as she rose and hugged each of her parents. For the past five years, she'd been content to blend into her East Coast fishing community. And now that she was a member of a clandestine merrow organization, she would be broadcasting her status as a princess of the sea. She could not decide whether she was pleased or terrified. Or both.

Chapter 2 –
Merrowmind Council

THE BRUSH-COVERED HILLS above the village made an ideal playground and browsing for goats. Rock outcrops protruded from the foliage except where they ended in solid cliffs overlooking rough beaches below. Further inland, the brush and sparse grass gave way to a forest of mixed hardwoods and evergreens. The scenery was not much different from Hildaland, the original home of the most senior does.

In spite of space limitations on the rescue ships, Jimmy had insisted that at least half his goats come with him when he left that prison island. The rest would continue to provide milk for the residents who refused to leave. As much as he loved each of the goats, Jimmy did not argue. He looked forward to introducing new genetic lines to his core herd when he established himself on the mainland. In fact, he suggested that they send some new breeding stock back to Hildaland, though no one had volunteered to make that trip again since they had left five years ago.

Kira and Jimmy sat on one of the cliff edges, their legs dangling over the side. The drop to the beach at this point was only five feet, a jump the goats often made just for fun. They would leap down, prance in a circle or to the surf's edge, then bounce back to the cliff, and, with a spring, scramble to the top again, over and over again.

"D-do you not want to go back there? Even for a look?" Jimmy asked.

"I don't think so," Kira replied. "First of all, the palace is crawling with finfolk, the whole area in fact. And second, I hear they've wrecked the place. It's a mess. Chris and Martin were there last month and reported what they saw to the Merrowmind Council. I'd be so depressed to see what they've done to Merhaven. I guess the finfolk chased off the merrows who used to live there. Who knows where they ended up." Kira drove her heels hard into the cliff face and watched her feet rebound. She was picturing the kind old maid who had helped her escape Merhaven. Was she still there, trapped and enslaved by the finfolk who had taken over?

"But the council is t-talking about taking it back. Putting a run to the f-finfolk."

"Sure, but that will take a lot of organizing, and it's going to be dangerous. It's on the agenda for the meeting tomorrow, my first one. I'm nervous."

Jimmy laughed. "N-not you, Miss Kira! You are the princess. They are your subjects." Since Jimmy had left Hildaland, his stutter had almost disappeared, except when he got excited.

"Princess, shmincess!" she said. "I don't feel like a princess. I can't see myself living in Merhaven, having servants all around me. It's just not me. I want to do something useful with my life."

"You have already done that, Miss Kira. You freed us from slavery, remember?" Jimmy smiled shyly.

"Jimmy, please. First, I had a lot of help getting you off Hildaland. I could never have done it alone. And second, stop calling me 'Miss Kira'! I'm just plain 'Kira,' okay?" She tried a stern face, but Jimmy shook his head.

"If you do not feel like a princess, I do not have to listen to you, *Miss* Kira." With a wide grin, he sprang to his feet and started whistling for the goats. "And since I am your boss this summer, I can tell you to go back to work." He pointed to his wrist as if he wore a watch. Jimmy worked on animal timetables.

"All right, Mr. Boss, I'm on my way!" Kira laughed as she trotted off toward the creamery, following the well-worn goat path back to the village.

***

"CALL TO ORDER!" Curtis Morgan called out, tapping an odd-shaped gavel on an upturned metal pan. The end of the gavel looked like a coneflower with drooping petals, but it was obviously made of a hard material. The clanging eventually stopped all conversations in the room. They sat tucked into Fred Gimli's living room, nine men and three women. Fred was the only human in the group; his mermaid wife, Cyndi, was not home for the meeting. Lamps had been lit and curtains drawn against casual glances through the windows from outside. The fishers of the group were already stifling yawns, having been up well before sunrise.

Kira scanned the faces around the room and found four she did not recognize, one of them rather young, perhaps in his early twenties. Merrows from nearby towns, she assumed. Kira sat to Currin's right while Borin stood at his left side. She'd been surprised to learn that her cousin was a member of the council. After his recent outburst, she couldn't help but worry that he may have a divided, or even a false, loyalty to the merrow half of his ancestry. She would have to discuss this with Currin when they were alone. At the same time, she was encouraged to see Ginny and Margaret representing the female contingent, since tradition held that only mermen attended such meetings. But those traditions had been disrupted when the merrows moved onto land. On top of that, landed mermaids outnumbered mermen by ten to one.

"Thank you, merrow folk and friends," Curtis continued. "Today we will begin by welcoming a new member to the Merrowmind Council, known to most of you as Miss Kira Cox. But in truth, she is the daughter of His Royal Highness, Currin Corinalis of Atlanta Maris." He waved his arm at Currin, who gave a brief nod. "I'm sure you are also aware of her role in freeing the prisoners of Hildaland." A round of applause erupted, and Curtis joined in, grinning. He and Fred were part of the force that had liberated the captives.

Kira wished she could disappear right then and was thankful for the dim lighting that hid her burning red face. What had she gotten herself into? She hoped this part of the meeting would pass quickly.

"Welcome, Kira!" Curtis boomed, followed by another burst of clapping. "It is most appropriate that Kira be here tonight for our discussion of reclaiming her hereditary home, Merhaven. As most of you know, we've had intelligence of increasing destruction of Merhaven and the surrounding area." He acknowledged Chris with a nod. "It seems the occupiers may be building some sort of processing centre next to Merhaven. Their buildings resemble the mayhem of an eagle's nest, but far worse. Made of scrap metal, wire, stones, broken bricks, plastic, whatever garbage they can scrounge from the ocean floor. Sadly, there is a lot of garbage to choose from, thanks to humans." Curtis looked apologetically at their host, standing by the door to the kitchen.

Fred smiled and shook his head. "It's okay. I totally agree with you. We are world-class producers of garbage and pollution."

"Anyway, ever since we drove them off Hildaland and welcomed many fine merrow folk who now live among us, there has been talk of routing the finfolk from Merhaven as well. Although we would welcome the chance to face them in the sea, most of us cannot do so. There are too few young merrows to take them on, and we would never send our children to war."

At the last words, Kira's heart sped up. War. They were talking about taking violent action against the finfolk.

"We need to find other merrows who still live in these seas, who still care about the Atlantic merrow communities, about our traditions. And most important, about stopping the spread of these aggressive finfolk." He turned to look at the young stranger, who, like Curtis, kept his thick dark-gold hair long and tied back in a ponytail. "Janus, you've seen more of the Atlantic than most of us. Do you think we can find sympathetic merrows to help us defeat the occupiers?"

Janus leaned forward into the light and brought his hand to his chin. Kira inhaled sharply. Just what Cody would do when deep in thought. Janus had a heavy brow, high cheekbones, a chiselled jaw. He reminded Kira of a handsome Mi'kmaq boy who had lived in their village for a few years but left with his family last summer.

"It is possible," he finally said. "I spent time with different communities on my way from Denmark before I landed on this coast. You have to be careful. Some are not so friendly. This I knew before I left, before I went back to the sea. But others, I think, might help us." He paused to rub his chin again.

Kira had never heard an accent like his. Danish influence, she supposed. His voice was rather pleasant to listen to, tinkling and chantlike. She wondered about his story, why he left Denmark, how he knew about unfriendly merrows. Maybe they were morphed finfolk, like Shree.

"I don't think you should travel alone, Janus. Perhaps we can find one or two merrows to go with you on this mission." Curtis looked around the room.

Borin cleared his throat, and Kira wondered whether he was about to volunteer. "What about Kira?"

She sat up straight and stared at him. He was volunteering *her*?

The nerve!

He continued, "You know, the help that Kira rounded up to storm Hildaland? Dolphins, giant octopuses, whales, whatever. What do you think, Kira?" Borin turned to meet her stare.

"I… I suppose," she began, "but it's not something I'm comfortable asking. This isn't their quarrel. It's not like Hildaland. There aren't captives or slaves to rescue." Kira's hands were trembling. She was so angry at Borin for putting her on the spot.

"Actually, we did see a couple of merrows at Merhaven," Chris said.

Currin jumped in. "They may not be what you think, Chris. As Janus pointed out, they could be enemy merrows. Or morphed finfolk."

Kira was grateful he spoke up before she did. She avoided looking at Borin and wondered how he felt at that moment, knowing his own mother was a morphed finfolk pretending to be a merrow. Of course, Shree may have dropped her disguise now that her own kind inhabited the merrow palace.

"I'll go with Janus!" Two voices, two arms raised at the same time. Chris and Borin stood up, and everyone clapped, including a relieved Kira. Perhaps this was Borin's way of making amends. Or acting as a spy. Kira felt badly that she mistrusted her cousin so much. She needed reassurance from Currin. He and Borin had grown close over the past five years.

Maybe it wouldn't hurt to call on her dolphin friends, even just to see how they were doing. They would tell her if anything else was going on that she should know about, near Merhaven in particular.

Curtis called for order, and they moved on to other agenda items, such as the new road proposal for their stretch of coastal villages. As they wrapped up the meeting, Cyndi walked in balancing a tray heaped with small tuna sandwiches and lemon squares. Tea and coffee were being served in the kitchen. Apparently, she'd just returned from a visit with Bess, Kira's mother.

Kira noticed Janus, Borin, and Chris huddled in a corner and wished she could overhear their conversation. She turned for the kitchen and found herself facing the other three merrows she had not met yet. They introduced themselves as fishers from up the shore, and each vigorously shook her hand while thanking her for her help at Hildaland. They had been among the captive merrows she helped release. Again, she felt embarrassed with their attention and praise. She was relieved when they excused themselves to return home for an early start the next morning.

"Come along, Janus! The bus is leaving," one of them called out. The young man shook hands with his two fellow volunteers and thanked Cyndi for the treats on his way out. He nodded at Kira as he was about to pass by but then stopped and held out his hand. She held hers out to shake.

"It would be a great pleasure to talk to you about your interesting adventures. If this can be arranged sometime," he said with a warm smile, bowing his head.

"Uh, sure. Let us know when you're back this way," Kira said.

"Yes, of course." He nodded and left.

Kira stood rooted, still seeing his bright white teeth and his dark-brown eyes like the emblazoned image of a Cheshire cat. Or were his eyes dark green? Unusual colour, she thought. Typical of Danish merrows, perhaps?

"Kira." Borin stepped in front of her, displacing Janus's face. In some ways, their features were not so different, except that Borin rarely cracked a smile, especially in her presence.

"So, Borin, you've signed up for a mission. That's great." She didn't know what else to say.

"Yeah, great. Something useful for a change. Anyway, none of us really know this Janus dude, so I'll be keeping an eye on him."

Kira stared at her cousin in disbelief. She realized she didn't know Borin all that well, either. "Right. And I could do some reconnaissance, too. Check in with my sea pals. They might have seen something that would be useful to us."

"Yeah. So, Janus said he wants to talk to you sometime. Maybe he thinks he has to ask male relatives for permission or something. I don't know how they do these things in Europe."

Kira blushed. "Oh, he just wants to talk about my undersea adventures."

"Uh, no, I think it's more than that. I'd watch out if I were you. He seems a bit slick to me."

"Maybe that's how they are in Denmark—uberpolite. More formal than here in the middle of nowhere."

"Maybe. Chris and I will find out more when we meet with him next week."

"Ready to head off, you two?" Currin had appeared from the kitchen.

After thanking their hosts and saying goodbye to the others, Kira and Borin followed Currin outside. They walked Kira to her door and left for their house on the other side of the village.

***

KIRA COLLAPSED INTO BED. What a crazy few days. Just when she thought she'd have a long, boring summer ahead, she was preparing for a clandestine underwater war. Cody would love this, she thought, all the strategic planning and preparation. But Cody wasn't here; he had his own life and projects now. And she had her own people to work with, the merrows. She clutched the warm Pendright in her hand, felt the metal spikes, sharp but soft at the same time, like pointed petals. Aha, the gavel! The same shape as her Pendright, of course.

Once again, she was in the thick of things, but she wasn't alone. This time she'd have support from the council and the entire merrow community. She closed her eyes and saw the dazzling smile again, the dancing dark eyes. A handsome, mysterious, exotic merrow wanted to meet with her. Now that was something to dream about.

Chapter 3 –
Janus

Over the next few days, Kira grew more restless and anxious about the plans to invade Merhaven. She said little about the council meeting to Bess and Cillian, except that she'd been embarrassed with all the attention when she'd been welcomed into the fold. She did not wish to worry her parents. Eventually, they would find out. Bess and Calista had become close friends, having so much in common, both were landed mermaids and adoptive parents. And they shared a daughter: Kira.

She couldn't stop thinking about Janus, wondering about his life story. Would he call her or try to find her when he came to town to meet with Borin and Chris?

Kira was washing dishes a week later when Bess came into the kitchen with the phone in her hand. "Call for you, Kira," she said, her eyebrows raised. "I don't know who it is."

"Oh?" Kira did not wish to venture a guess, but her heart was racing. She took the phone. "Hello, this is Kira."

"Kira. This is Janus speaking," he said in his singsong voice. "Is it a good time to talk?"

"Uh, sure," she replied, her face hot. What was wrong with her?

"We are just now finishing our discussions, and I wondered if you and I could meet somewhere? If you are free?"

"Uh, yeah. Would you like to come here, to my house? We could take a walk along the beach."

"Yes, that would be suitable. Borin can tell me where to find you, yes?"

"He knows where I live. Where are you now?"

"At the café in town."

"Oh, the Bayview Diner?"

"Yes, that one. Shall I come now, if it is convenient?"

"Now is a good time. We just finished dinner."

"I will see you soon. Goodbye."

"Bye."

Her heart rate was gradually slowing down. She had just invited a perfect stranger to her home. The diner wasn't far, and Janus could be there within ten minutes. She finished the dishes and then ran to her room to change, glad her parents hadn't asked whom she'd been talking to. She struggled out of her work T-shirt and quickly slipped on a black tank top and cutoff jean shorts. At seven o'clock it was still warm outside, even with the stiff breeze whipping in off the water.

When Kira heard the knock, she raced to the door before her parents could rise out of their comfy chairs in the living room. She was surprised to see two people at the door, Janus and Borin. Before she could speak, Cillian's voice boomed out from behind her.

"Borin! Nice to see you. And you brought a friend, I see." His big, friendly arm thrust out past Kira to shake Borin's hand.

"Hello, Cillian. And Mrs. Cox. This here is Janus. A new friend of mine from Brookvale, up the shore."

"I am pleased to meet you," Janus spoke, putting out his hand for introductions.

Kira listened nervously while Borin explained that Janus was working at the packing plant and had recently arrived from Denmark. He had heard about Kira and wanted to meet her.

Bess appraised Janus and asked, point-blank, "Oh, what have you heard about her?" She smiled, but her eyes were narrowed.

Janus flashed his brilliant smile at her. "Ah, she is famous. What she has done for the merrows here. This news travels far. I am most honoured to meet her." He held his hand out to Kira, who shook it, somewhat dazed. She could feel her parents relaxing a little, for now they knew he was a merrow.

"So, we thought we'd go for a walk along the beach," Borin said before they could be invited inside.

"Indeed, a lovely evening for a walk," Cillian said. "You're welcome to come in afterward, if you like."

The three of them hurried off down the hill, over the rocks to the beach. There was a narrow strip of sand between the water and rocks at low tide where they walked, south, away from the village. No one spoke for a long time. Kira wondered if Borin intended to stay or leave at some point. This was supposed to be a meeting between her and Janus, wasn't it?

"So, Kira, Janus was telling us that he's done a lot of undersea travelling, across the Atlantic, up and down the coasts. Met a lot of merrows and some finfolk, too."

Janus nodded his head but remained silent.

"Why did you leave Denmark, Janus? Were those your home waters?" Kira asked, still irked that Borin was tagging along.

"Yes," he said, looking at Kira briefly before staring straight ahead. "My parents were both killed in a fight with local finfolk. I think these monsters are bigger and fiercer on the European side of the Atlantic. They are determined to exterminate all merrows. This is why we must not let them bully you here, also."

"How old were you?" Kira asked.

"I was about seven years old. Like you, Kira, I came out of the sea to live with a family on land. They were farmers, farther inland. I did not enjoy working on the farm. My step-parents were not unkind, but it was not a life I wished to choose. So, when I was eighteen, I returned to the sea." He turned his head and smiled at Kira.

"And now here I am, and I wish to help you chase away these evil finfolk. Borin and Chris and I will look for other merrows to join us," he said, grinning at Borin.

"Did you see the fight? Were you there when it happened?" Borin asked. Kira shot a tight-lipped frown at her cousin.

Janus nodded and then turned to look at Kira, his face grim. "Yes, I was close enough to see the attack, but far enough away for me to swim to shore where they could not catch me. I ran and ran. I don't know how long. My feet were bleeding when I stopped, and some local people found me and took pity."

"You mentioned unfriendly merrows, too," Kira said. "What were they like?"

"Ah yes, I remember them from when I was young. I believe they had come from the north, beyond the Finnish waters. They had different scales, all shades of green, narrower than ours, and their jaws were more pointed. I used to play with the younger ones. They were fast and liked to ram into each other and us. My parents called them uncivilized. Before my parents were ambushed, they had a terrible quarrel with this tribe. I do not know if they had anything to do with the attack, but I never saw them again."

All three had stopped by then, having moved up onto the rocks as the tide crept higher and swallowed the sand.

"You see, Kira, we are alike. We are victims of the finfolk. Except your parents survived. Now it is up to us, we who can return to the sea, to free your kingdom from these thieves and murderers." He leaned toward Kira and touched her arm briefly—just long enough to give her chills, followed by a heat wave.

Kira turned toward the water so they couldn't see her flushed face. "Yes, it's time to take back what is ours," she agreed. "While you are out looking for merrows to join us, I'll call on my other friends."

As they resumed walking, Janus said, "Now Kira, you must tell me more about yourself. You are famous in the merrow world, you know. A most unusual mermaid." Again, that brilliant smile.

"Guys," Borin interrupted, "I've gotta go. I have a project deadline. Janus, you've got a ride back to Brookvale, right? At nine-thirty?"

"That is correct. Thank you, my friend, for the meeting and bringing me here. I will see you soon, yes?"

"You bet. Next Saturday, dive day! Later, Kira." He waved a hand at her without meeting her eyes and left, hopping from rock to rock like they were molten lava.

That was a surefire way to get rid of him, Kira thought. He hated hearing about her brave deeds, as he put it—the adventures that had evicted him from his cozy home in Merhaven, landed him on a prison island, and then sentenced him to life on the mainland. She was sorry he felt that way, but she was not sorry that he had left her alone with Janus.

As much as she did not feel comfortable recounting her life story, Janus put her at ease with his smiles and prompting. By the time they had returned to her house, it was dark, and he had to hurry off to meet the fisher who would take him back to Brookvale.

He stood at the door to her house and took her hand, raised it to his lips, and kissed it. "I hope I can meet with you again, Princess Kira." His smile was mischievous and warm.

Kira had stopped breathing for a moment. "Oh, go on with you," she said, laughing. And then, in case he didn't understand her meaning, she added, "I'm sure we will meet again. Good luck on your mission, and please be careful."

With that, he saluted her and disappeared into the dark.

The house was also dark inside. Cillian went to bed early during fishing season, and Bess wasn't far behind, as she worked early shifts at the diner. Kira needed to talk to someone, to tell them about Janus, the mysterious stranger with the gorgeous smile, the lovely Danish accent, and quaint manners. She'd never met a true foreigner before. She'd never felt her heart do flip-flops before, either. He'd kissed her hand! Such a simple gesture, yet so thrilling.

Many of the girls at school had boyfriends, and she knew they had been intimate with them, kissing and well beyond. Two of them had left school to have babies, long before they graduated. Kira knew all about the facts of life but had no close girlfriends with whom to share her own romantic discoveries and feelings. Bess was the closest to being a confidante, followed by Calista and Amelie. Then there was dear Jimmy, but she could never discuss matters of the heart with him; he'd be mortified. Maybe Ginny? No, she was a committed gossip.

Kira used to share everything with Cody. She shuddered and felt a heaviness in her stomach. She missed Cody so much. He should be here. What would he think of Janus? Would he be suspicious like Borin, or would he be curious and want to interrogate the Danish merrow about details of life in European waters, their diet, and any technology they had developed? She was certain Cody would be on board with their plans to oust the finfolk and permanently evict them from Merhaven. But no, he would have no interest in Kira's love life. Anyway, it would be just plain weird to even discuss such things with him. He was gone. She'd have to deal with all these new feelings on her own. She was her own person, making her own way. And one of those paths would lead her back into the ocean.

Chapter 4 –
Reconnaissance

THE NEXT DAY OFF WORK, Kira informed her parents that she was going to pay a visit to old friends and not to expect her back for supper. And maybe longer. They understood. Kira periodically returned to the sea to find a certain pod of dolphins that travelled just off their coast. They never tried to stop her. They could also not stop worrying about her when she was off by herself, but they knew she was careful and that her undersea friends were watching out for her.

Unlike many teenagers, Kira was happy to be up early in the morning. Even so, her parents were away at work before she arose. On this summer morning, the sun was barely above the water, and the surface glimmered silver and gold. Kira stood for a moment on the sandy beach, barefoot, enjoying the cold-water massage as the waves lapped over her feet. The ocean seemed so innocent and calm at that interface of air and water. Gulls were crying above, insects were singing and scurrying in the sand and rocks, and squirrels were chattering in the trees. Underneath, the sea was swarming with microscopic, nearly invisible creatures as well as animals the size of football stadiums. That was where she was headed, to navigate between the benign and the plundering citizens of the sea.

As soon as she dove in, she was fully at home, her streamlined merrow body slipping through the water with the mere flick of her royal purple tail. She looked back to admire her shining golden scales with the pink stripe along each side, now fuchsia-coloured under the morning sun streaming through the water. Her first immersion in the sea since Currin had presented her with the Pendright. Kira felt for the silver and gold pendant where it hung from her neck. As Calista had predicted, it was firmly adhered to and integrated with her chest scales. It was part of her merrow armour now.

Kira had several methods for tracking the dolphin pod. If she were in no hurry, she would swim in random patterns and enjoy the scenery while listening for their distinctive squeaks and whistles. If she had limited time but no sense of real urgency, she would sweep back and forth along the coast, slipping deeper into the ocean with each pass. However, if she were in trouble and needed their help immediately, she would send a distress call. This was not such a day. She never considered calling out in jest. A false call for aid would be rude and disturbing. They would recognize her voice, and she didn't wish to alarm them. Anyway, she did not want to be the first merrow to cry wolf in the sea.

Today she simply enjoyed flying through the water, observing the beauty of the sea, its plants and colourful inhabitants, the aquatic tones and soothing sounds that let her know all was well beneath the waves. Even so, she studied the movements of small and medium-sized fish for clues. Dolphins spent a lot of time feeding. "Follow the fish, find the dolphins," they had advised her, and then they laughed. Their sense of humour was the feature that Kira most appreciated after their loyalty to family and friends.

Though he could not understand their language, Cody had desperately wanted to see for himself how dolphins laughed. Dolphins express laughter with their entire bodies since they can't move the muscles around their mouths and eyes as humans do. When Cody took up scuba diving, he finally got his wish. Watching them laugh, Cody couldn't help but succumb to his own full-body convulsions of joy and what sounded like hiccups to Kira. That in turn made the dolphins hysterical as they swam wild circles around him, squeaking and bumping him gently from time to time. They admitted to Kira that Cody was the first human they actually liked and fully trusted. Secretly, the compliment made her happy and proud of him, as if he had passed a critical test of seaworthiness.

What she noticed this morning was that the fish farther offshore seemed in greater disarray and more frantic than usual. Had the pod just passed this way? She heard no distinctive dolphin vocalizations, so they were not nearby. Something had clearly disturbed the fish. Perhaps a fishing boat or a smaller, faster craft with a loud motor. Kira sensed that the disturbance had occurred farther out and north, so she changed course to swim in that direction. She decided to keep a lower profile and hugged the seabed, where she could hide quickly if she wished. Sneaking up on a pod of dolphins or a herd of seals was no easy task, but she would love to pull it off if she could. That would be a coup; they were constantly doing it to her.

A small school of fish appeared above her and then flashed off. She peered into the blackness of the sea from where they had come and saw a large, dark object approaching at great speed. As it grew nearer, Kira could make out a pointed snout and a large rounded back with spiky fins. Suddenly the silvery blue fish was above and shooting past her in the direction of the small school. A spectacular bluefin tuna! She had never seen one before. They were a rare sight in these waters. She hoped that the giant beauty would not be tempted by any long lines and hooks of local tuna fishers.

She had stopped and was looking into the distant indigo darkness where the tuna had disappeared when a larger school of fish zoomed by above her. She turned around and froze at what she saw. A cluster of large oddly shaped fish was approaching from where all the other fish had come, swimming lower down and more slowly than the tuna.

She flattened herself onto the sea floor and remained absolutely still. This group was not a typical school of fish or a herd of seals or a pod of dolphins. Kira shuddered, praying it wasn't a group of finfolk, either. As their features came into focus, it was clear they were none of these. They each held long, narrow objects in their hands. Human divers? No, merrows!

Kira could not tell if they had seen her. At such a moment, she wished her scales were dull so they would blend with the background. Better yet, she would have loved the octopus's ability to change colours and be perfectly camouflaged. She tried to calm herself. They were merrows, after all, and she should have nothing to fear from them. Instinctively, her hand reached up to cover her shining Pendright.

At that same moment, she knew she had been spotted. The group of merrows slowed and approached her, sinking down so they hovered, facing her in a semicircle. They were not local merrows. They were larger, their scales shimmered in hues of green, their skin was olive, and their long, clumped hair was a rusty brown. However, Kira was most disturbed by the long barbed spears that each merrow held. The closest one stared at her with his hooded eyes and spoke.

"Ta chapla dizz hunbin," was what Kira thought she heard.

"I'm sorry, I don't understand you." Kira was nervous. The only other merrow-like creatures she had ever met that she could not understand were finfolk.

The speaker waved his spear in the direction of the tuna that had passed by. Then he pointed at Kira.

"Ta chapla korgun!"

With one hand still covering the Pendright, Kira pointed her free hand in the direction of the tuna. "That way, it went that way!" She tried to read the expression on his face. She could not discern if he was angry, impatient, or confused. She wondered how far they could throw those spears. A distress call was out of the question. Dolphins could become the targets of these hunters.

The foreign merrows grumbled to each other, shaking their spears and shooting dark looks at Kira. She hoped they didn't notice her trembling. She tensed herself, prepared to push off if she needed to escape. Finally, the strangers turned away, facing the direction of the tuna trail. With two beats of their muscular tails, they were gone, disappearing into the deep blue in pursuit of their quarry. Kira did not budge until they had disappeared from sight. Then she rocketed up and raced off in the opposite direction. When she felt she was far enough, she made her call: *"EEE-U-EEE-U-EEE!"*

Kira sank to the bottom again and rested next to an outcrop of rock, making herself as small as possible. In all the years she had been cruising underwater along these shores, she had never seen such unusual and unfriendly merrows. Was there a connection with Janus, who had just described such merrows from northern Europe? Or was it a coincidence? She wondered what *he* looked like underwater. Chris and Borin would see for themselves tomorrow. Should she warn them? But that was crazy. Janus didn't look anything like these merrows: his skin was fair; his hair, honey coloured; and his eyes… Kira stopped to think. Dark green? Brown? Why couldn't she remember?

And as for Borin, she still wasn't sure about him. Maybe she should talk to Chris alone. He was dependable and honest, and the entire community, merrows and humans, thought very highly of him. Then again, if she kept this information from Borin and shared it with Chris, Borin would know she didn't trust him. They didn't have the best relationship to start with, and perhaps that wouldn't change anything anyway. But then Chris would wonder about her. Why were things so complicated?

"Whee!"

Kira looked up to find Cass's beak in her face. She immediately threw her arms around his neck, or she tried to. Cass was a mature male dolphin now, nearly as dark as his father, Steen, and definitely more muscular. Kira's arms barely reached around Cass's body.

Cass began to convulse, and Kira let go, laughing with him. "Thanks for coming, Cass. And you too, Rom and Tork. I'm saved again!"

Cass spun around her. "What did we save you from this time, Princess?" He cocked his head at her, pretending to look stern.

What *had* he saved her from? "Hunters, strange merrows with spears. They didn't hurt me, but they were not friendly. So I wanted to warn you."

"Ah, those merrows. Yes, we have seen them, and we keep our distance. They like to hunt big fish and small octopuses," Cass said.

"No, not octopuses!" Kira was repulsed and upset. How could anyone hunt and kill such intelligent, sensitive creatures? Granted, they were not all the same and were very different from their giant cousins—nothing like Sherman and his family, except they were the same species.

"*Chk, chk*, Kira," said Cass, trying to imitate her chiding tsk sound. "Some merrows of your tribe eat the little eight-armed heads. I tried once, but I didn't like the arms trying to crawl out of my mouth!" He laughed and was rewarded by body slams from his two companions, the equivalent of human high-fives.

"Stop! You guys are awful!" She tried to slap Cass's tail as he slipped by her, but she missed.

"Seriously, Cass, how long have you known about these merrows? How long have they been here?"

"Maybe one, maybe two moon cycles."

"There were four males in the group I met. They were following a large tuna. And fast. I've never seen such fast and strong merrows."

"But not faster than the tuna. These merrows are like humans. They are greedy and take more fish than they can eat. We have seen no others like them, no females or young, just these hunters." Cass and Rom shook their heads in dismay.

Tork had swum off shortly after they had arrived, to let the pod know that Kira was safe. This was standard operating procedure for the dolphin clan when it came to Kira. Now the two others escorted her between them, swimming toward the pod. "Only the four merrows, no other hunters like them?" she asked.

"None that we have seen," Rom answered.

"Have you spoken to them?"

Cass laughed. "No. They do not approach us, and we do not tempt merrows with weapons. Even I have no desire to play such games."

Cass had certainly matured since Kira first met him as a mischievous youngster several years ago. He took many risks back then, much to the consternation of his father, Steen. That bold behaviour got him trapped in a fishnet, and that was how she met Cass and his pod and why they became lifelong friends.

"How is your father, Cass?" she asked.

"He is well, and here he is now." Within seconds Kira was in the midst of the pod, with younger dolphins whizzing around her squeaking and clicking and blowing bubbles, their usual happy greeting when they had not seen her in some time. Once they had all danced and played, the young ones were escorted away while Kira conferred with the elders.

She described to Steen her encounter with the foreign merrow hunters on her way to find their pod and then explained the purpose of her trip. "We learned that the finfolk had taken over Merhaven not long ago," she said. "The Merrowmind Council has decided to reclaim our home and territory and to remove the finfolk invaders.

I am here to ask if you have seen or know anything that we should know before we proceed with our plans."

Kira had thought ahead about how she would word her request. Although the dolphins were her personal friends, she knew they did not like to interfere in human or merrow matters. Nonetheless, a few of them had been drawn into the storming of Hildaland to free the human and merrow slaves, which included Kira's parents.

"Princess Kira, we have been watching, and we are concerned with how close the finfolk have come to our own territory. Dolphin families have their own system of which feeding grounds they use and live in. We find ourselves losing space on all sides. The arrival of new, aggressive merrows is also a worry. We wonder why they have come. Are they only searching for food, or are they here for other purposes? They are never separated from their weapons."

Kira sensed Steen's apprehension and her own anxiety level shot up. "Tomorrow my cousin and two other merrows will be travelling farther out, searching for merrows who might be willing to join us in our action against the finfolk. It might be wise for them to carry weapons also. But that may give friendly merrows the wrong impression."

Steen nodded, something he did for Kira's benefit. "We cannot fight the finfolk, but we also wish them gone from our waters. Let us know when your plans are in place. Our young must be hidden and well away from any harm. Then we will be ready to assist if there is anything we can do."

Kira bowed her head and thanked him, holding back the urge to give him a hug.

"I notice you wear the royal symbol of your merrow clan, Princess. We are honoured to be allies with you. But select your own allies carefully. If we have to choose, we will protect our own families first."

"Of course you must!" After a further exchange of news both above and below the water, Kira waved farewell and left the pod, but not without her escort of three dolphin chums. She seized the chance to grill them further.

"What Father did not tell you," Cass began, "is that we have been monitoring finfolk activity since they moved in. Father is more worried than he lets on. We think they have been digging tunnels out of Merhaven, but we aren't sure where to. So we have dolphins looking for them around Merhaven. There aren't enough of us to cover the whole area, though."

"Do you think they suspect an invasion?"

"They are clever. We don't know if their behaviour is normal or extra defensive. There still are two or three merrows at the palace. If we could talk to them, maybe we could find out. But we can't get close without serving ourselves up for their dinner!"

"Nor would I encourage you to do so! Some finfolk can shapeshift into merrow form, so you can never be sure who you are dealing with." Kira, of course, was thinking of Shree. Her disguise and guile were good enough to fool Nim, though perhaps he wasn't the brightest light in the palace.

By the time Kira was home again, she knew she had to talk to Borin and Chris before they headed out the next morning.

"Hello, Amelie? It's Kira. Is Borin home?" she blurted, breathless, dropping her usual pleasantries and chitchat. She winced, remembering how sensitive Amelie could be to voice tone.

"No, he isn't. I haven't seen him all day."

"Could you have him call me when he gets in?"

"Sure. But it won't be for a while."

"Do you know when he'll be back?"

"Uh, not really. Calista said he was off on a field trip or something and might not be back for a few days."

"What? He's gone already? Are you sure?"

"Yeah, I think so. He wasn't here when I got up this morning, and he always sleeps in on Saturdays when he can."

"Oh no."

"What's the matter?"

"Uh, nothing. I just wanted to tell him something, nothing important. It can wait till he's back," Kira lied and then stomped her foot in frustration. She heard a peal of girlish laughter in the background. "Sounds like you have company, Amelie."

"Oh, it's just Laurie and Margie. We're making a pizza tonight while the grown-ups are out visiting. Don't worry, everything is under control," she laughed.

Kira sighed. "I'm sure it is. Have fun!"

"Okay, bye."

"Damn!" There was no one to call, no way to get the message to Borin, Chris, and Janus. Even if she went back to the sea to look for them, they had at least fourteen hours on her. She tried to calm herself, rationalizing that the four merrow hunters had not harmed her. Three adult males should be able to take care of themselves. After all, Janus had travelled across and around the Atlantic Ocean, all on his own. There was no good reason to worry, was there?

Chapter 5 –
Strange Alliance

EARLY THE NEXT MORNING, Kira walked to Currin and Calista's house to share what she had learned. Calista's eyebrows shot up momentarily on hearing the news, though Currin did not appear concerned.

"There are many different tribes of merrows in the world's oceans," he said. "Most of them we only know about through stories passed down to us. Like humans, we have evolved to fit the environments where we live. Perhaps we developed fewer variations than land dwellers because the oceans do not have the same extremes of climate. I have met merrows from the southern and central Atlantic during my own explorations as a youngster. Much to my mother's disapproval," he added, chuckling.

Kira perked up. She had not thought much about merrows in other parts of the world until she'd met Janus. People in the coastal communities did not vary much in appearance, though she was aware of the many human races that existed on the planet. "So, what are they like, these other merrow tribes?"

"The central Atlantic tribes are not much different from us. Our clans mostly have silver or grey scales. Their scales are greyish blue. Within each tribe, certain lines, like our family, have gold or bronze scales. The central Atlantic merrows' hair is much like ours—brown, blond, some red. Their bodies are perhaps slightly broader and larger. But the southern merrows, they really stand out. Their scales are bright silver, and their bodies are longer and more slender. The tail fins have long thin tips that give the impression of trailing filaments.

And the tails are coloured gold and green, sometimes bright blue. Very attractive, I thought."

"Hmph!"

Currin laughed at his wife. "You had to see them, Calista. They flashed in the sunlight near the surface. Useful, too. Those glittering tails attracted lots of fish and made feeding time so much easier for the southern merrows."

"Currin! That's terrible," Calista laughed. "Perhaps they attracted more than fish, Currin. You didn't tempt any mermaids to follow you back north?"

"Oh, the thought crossed my mind, being young and full of myself at the time. But they would not have enjoyed the water here, far too cold for them. And I could not remain long in their tepid waters!"

"Indeed, I'm sure it was hot down there," Calista teased.

"But what were they like?" Kira asked. "I mean, were they friendly? Did they have different customs? Where did they live?"

"Their dwellings were similar to ours, except they also used living coral in their walls. If the homes were large enough, they would build around the coral to include it in their gardens. They were very careful not to disturb the living corals. I hear that many of the corals are dying now and losing their beautiful colours. Human pollution, of course. I suppose some of the merrows might have moved since then, especially if the fish have left or are being poisoned."

"And the central Atlantic merrows?"

"Their homes are built like ours here. All the merrows I met were friendly and curious and eager to learn about us northerners. As for the northern European merrows, I never did see one myself, but our cousins from the central Atlantic told us that they are heavier, with scales in mottled green, and some of them are not particularly social. I think they may have harsher conditions to live in, though there is plenty to eat in their waters. But there is also more human activity."

"I remember reading about a harbour in Denmark where they have a statue of a mermaid. And they have stories about mermaids," Kira said. "Do you think the Danish people know about us?"

Calista answered, "I believe they did know about us at one time when it was perhaps safer to come out of the water. But things have changed, as you know."

Currin reached for the carafe of coffee on the table where they sat. "Refill, anyone?" Calista handed him her cup.

Kira watched their ritual, a regular Sunday morning in her other parents' kitchen, with the sun just rising outside. They seemed unconcerned about the fate of their nephew, somewhere in the Atlantic Ocean, searching for friendly merrow faces. Kira began to relax. They just had to wait until the scouting trio returned to learn how they fared on their mission.

***

SIX DAYS LATER, Kira got the call from Currin. "They've returned, Kira, safe and sound. They found what they were looking for!" he said, his voice pitched. "Can you come to a Merrowmind Council meeting tonight at Fred's?"

"Sure!"

Kira's curiosity made her feel like an overfilled hot-air balloon. She couldn't wait for her work shift to be over.

"Girl, what are you doing?" Ginny suddenly appeared at her side.

Kira looked at the mountain of sliced Gouda piled up in front of her. "Oh. Guess I got carried away."

"We'll never sell that much sliced cheese before it goes green. I suppose it will be mac and cheese all week for you and me, eh? It freezes well. Good thing you're so tight with Jimmy. Anyone else would be fired."

"Ha, Jimmy couldn't fire someone even if they really deserved to be booted out," Kira said, weighing out stacks of slices on wax paper and sliding them into bags.

"Uh-huh," Ginny said, her eyebrows raised. "So, what were you dreaming about? Maybe that new fella from Brookvale? Aha! You're blushing!"

"Ginny, give it a rest. You're always pairing people up and then breaking them up in your mind."

"Aw, honey, I know about the meeting tonight. Exciting news, eh? Most people around here don't have a clue about what's going on out there."

"And let's hope they never figure it out."

"Mm-hmm, my lips are sealed." Ginny laughed and pressed her lips together.

That evening, as everyone filed into Fred's living room, they were surprised to see a visitor sitting with Janus. Next to him were Chris and Borin, their heads together in a corner, deep in conversation while Janus appeared to be translating for the newcomer. Kira recognized him immediately. He was one of the merrow hunters, though not the one who had tried to communicate with her. His unruly hair hung nearly to his waist, and his ill-fitting shirt and pants were apparently borrowed. She tried not to stare at him, discreetly gauging his expression while Janus spoke to him.

Borin touched Janus's shoulder, and they both looked up at Kira across the room. Janus waved at her to approach. She walked over, assuming they wanted to introduce her to the stranger.

Janus said something to the merrow, who gave her a quick glance and nodded. "I just asked him if you were the mermaid they saw a few days ago. He says you were having some trouble."

"What? I wasn't in trouble," she said, her eyes wide.

Janus smiled. "He says they asked you if you were in trouble, and you told them to go away. He says you were not friendly, but I cannot believe that."

Kira's mouth dropped open. "Oh? What I saw were four large strangers approaching me, holding weapons. One of them pointed a spear at me and said something I couldn't make out. I told him I didn't understand what he said. He looked angry and pointed his spear in the direction of a large tuna that had just passed by. I also pointed that way and said that's where the tuna had gone. And off they went. I assumed they were hunting it."

Janus smiled at her. Kira continued, "Can you please explain that to him? I don't want any misunderstandings."

"No, of course not. I will translate for you." Kira listened to the strange language. It did not sound like any European language she had ever heard. Currin had never mentioned having difficulty understanding the other merrow tribes he had encountered.

A loud banging and call to order from Curtis cut off her thoughts. Kira found a place to sit across the room from Janus and company.

"Thank you for coming on short notice," Curtis said. "Our three courageous young men, Chris, Borin, and Janus, returned from their recruiting mission yesterday with excellent news. They covered a lot of territory and found many willing merrows, more than we'll need, really, to take Merhaven back from the finfolk." Before he could continue, loud cheering and applause broke out from all assembled, as well as from the kitchen, where a celebratory meal was being prepared.

"I have asked Chris to give us a report on their mission. Chris, the floor is yours."

Chris Miller, who, Kira figured, was about twenty-two years old, stood up and cleared his throat. He was part of the fourth generation of enslaved merrows rescued from Hildaland, one who had left his parents behind but had few regrets. And he'd had little trouble adapting to life in their village, eventually finding a job in the local fishery.

"We weren't out long, maybe six hours or so, before we ran into a group of merrows southeast of Bakers Island. Great fishing grounds, as we know. They have a nice life out there, and little trouble from finfolk, but they said they would sign up and help us. They know about Merhaven and Hildaland and have no love for these thieves and vandals. And it didn't hurt to have Borin with us since he's a nephew of King Currin. It means a lot to all merrows that the king and queen were found."

He paused a moment as several merrows murmured and nodded their heads. Kira was thinking how Borin might have felt, representing the royal family. She wasn't sure how she felt about that herself and wondered if she shouldn't have volunteered to travel with them as the heir to the throne and the palace. But then, that was a role she was not comfortable with.

"So, this clan told us about others who might be interested in sending a few of their experienced merrows to help with the fight, and before long, we had an army ready to go."

Kira shivered while another cheer went up from the crowd. An army? A fight? Why not? They had invaded Hildaland, prepared to fight the finfolk. But that was mainly on land. In the water, merrows were at a disadvantage because they did not normally use weapons, whereas finfolk were weaponized creatures with razor-sharp teeth and claws. They were also skilled at morphing into many shapes and disguises.

She looked up at the stranger with the sallow skin and pointed chin and shivered again. There was something unsettling about him.

In all this time, except for a few serious words with Janus, he had not opened his mouth or smiled. This was not surprising if he didn't understand English.

Once the room was quiet again, Chris continued. "We also came across a few members of a tribe from across the northern Atlantic, from near Iceland. Janus can tell you more about them." Chris sat down quickly, looking relieved to give up the floor.

Janus stood up and smiled broadly. "Thank you for your attention. Yes, this was a most fortunate meeting. Four nomadic hunters from the Spegar tribe have travelled here. They search for tuna and other large fish. They use spears to hunt and can train our merrows to use undersea weapons against finfolk if it becomes necessary. We know the finfolk can be fierce warriors, and most merrows do not have experience with military culture." He turned around and beckoned to the visitor to step forward, which he did.

"This is Krig. He is the youngest of the four and the only one who could come on land to meet with us." He turned to Krig and spoke a few words. Krig nodded at the council members and attempted a smile. More like a tight-lipped grimace, Kira thought. Perhaps that tribe never smiled, so maybe she had misinterpreted the mood of the one who had spoken to her.

Krig and Janus sat down. Curtis opened the floor to questions. Fred raised his hand. "So, do these northern merrows not understand any English?"

"That is correct," Janus replied. "I will translate for them."

"How will they teach the others to use weapons?"

"They will demonstrate their techniques, especially with spears," Janus said.

"What about spearguns?" Fred asked. "They would be more efficient and have a longer range than hand-held spears."

Chris spoke up. "We were discussing that, and because finfolk fight close up without weapons, a hand-held spear will keep them far enough away so they can't do any damage. These spears are lighter, longer, and easier to handle than a speargun. But they're strong enough that they won't break if one of the finfolk gets hold of the barbed end. They're amazing weapons. We got to try them out."

His enthusiasm was obvious. Kira wondered if being enslaved by the finfolk for the first seventeen years of his life was behind his motivation to fight them.

"I have a question," Curtis said. "How did they get these spears?"

"Yes, a good question. I also asked this. Krig says they are very old spears. His tribe has had them a long, long time. No one remembers where they came from. Perhaps a Viking warship that sank in a storm."

More questions followed, some of them technical, some tactical. As Kira listened, she watched Krig, trying to pinpoint what was bothering her. She simply didn't trust him. She worried that Chris was so eager to fight that he wasn't being critical enough. Janus seemed comfortable with Krig, so that was probably good enough for Chris. Perhaps Janus knew Krig from when he was young. What were the chances of that? She would ask him next time they were alone.

By the end of the evening, a schedule had been mapped out for Operation Free Merhaven. One of the spears would be used as a template to make more spears at a metal shop in Bevanton, a town about an hour's drive from the village. Fred and Currin would make those arrangements. Meanwhile, the Spegars would travel with Janus to the various locations where they would train volunteer merrows to use the spears in hand-to-hand combat, should that became necessary.

Kira offered to coordinate surveillance of finfolk activities around Merhaven between the dolphins and local merrow volunteers. She felt much better knowing she could contribute in some way, though she knew her parents Bess and Cillian might not be as keen.

Before Janus left the meeting with Krig, Kira got his attention and called him aside. "I'd like to speak to you sometime in private before you go on your training sessions," she said. "Will you have time?"

"Yes, of course, I would love to talk to you before we go. I will make the time for you," he said, touching her elbow briefly.

Kira willed her heart to stop racing. "Okay, tomorrow evening, around seven?"

"Yes, I will come to your house if that is acceptable?"

"Yes, see you then."

Janus gave her one of his bright smiles. Kira looked at his eyes before he turned away to leave, trying to determine the colour once and for all. In the dim lighting of the room, they appeared to be deep brown. She decided she would have to see him in bright daylight to know for sure. Why that was important, she didn't know.

***

THE NEXT EVENING Janus appeared at her door at one minute to seven o'clock.

"Please come in for a minute, Janus. My parents want to say hello," Kira said, opening the door wide.

He stepped inside and greeted Cillian and Bess, shaking hands again. They invited him to sit in the living room.

"So, Janus," Cillian began, "Kira tells us that you will help train peace-loving merrows to become warriors. That's quite an undertaking. My father was in the military for a while, a so-called peacekeeper in Africa. He saw some terrible things, but he was never allowed to fight. He came home a frustrated, bitter man."

Kira was surprised to hear her dad talking about his father, who was lost at sea during a wicked storm. He rarely ever mentioned him. Cillian had been one of the crew on that boat and always felt guilty that he had not been close enough to keep his father from going overboard.

"He refused to put on the floatation gear, stubborn old man. I've always wondered if he wanted to go, if he'd had enough."

Kira was shocked. She'd never heard him suggest that his father might have committed suicide.

"Young man, have you ever been near a battle or had to fight?"

Janus cleared his throat and looked down for a moment. "No, sir. Only one time, when my parents were attacked. They were ambushed, I think. They had no weapons, no way to defend themselves. I was very young. When my mother screamed at me to swim away, swim fast, not to look back, I did what she told me."

"And you never saw them again?" Bess asked, her voice quivering. She reached over to hold Kira's hand.

"No," Janus said, raising his head. "I waited on the beach, behind some bushes. They had prepared me for such a thing, and I followed their instructions. When some time passed and I did not see them, I began to run away from the water, far away, until I found help and people who took me in." He sighed deeply.

"So, you see, I have good reason to help this community in their fight. Finfolk are devious and ruthless, and we must have a strong force, willing to use weapons. It is not a pleasant thing, but they are the ones who have invaded your waters. And they are dangerous."

"And these Icelandic merrows, do you trust them?" Cillian asked. "I hear they are not very friendly."

Janus smiled. "No, they are not social like the rest of us, but they are not aggressive. They only use weapons to hunt. They were persuaded to help when they learned they were on other merrows' territories. Even in their society, it is a courtesy to ask permission before hunting in a new place. Also, they do not care for finfolk. I believe they have done battle with these evil creatures in the past."

By the time Kira and Janus left the house, she was happy for the fresh air outside. "Wow, that was heavy going. I'm sorry you had to bring up all that history. I think my dad was just very sad about his own father and what the war had done to him. He probably suffered from post-traumatic stress, but they didn't know much about it back then."

Janus reached for her hand as they walked, and Kira felt her entire body glow at his touch. "Are you okay?" she asked. "After what happened to you?"

"Ah, yes, I think so. It was so long ago. Sometimes it feels like I am telling a story about someone else, not me. But it did teach me to be careful, and watchful, and not to accept things as they appear to be." He squeezed her hand. "Kira, if I may be so bold to ask, would you come for a swim with me? I would love to see your beautiful golden scales." He stopped and gave her what looked like a shy smile.

"Or maybe you don't believe I am who I say I am?" she teased him.

"No!" he protested. "Have I offended you?"

"Come on! I'd love to go for a swim." Kira removed her shoes and glasses and ran into the surf. She dove in without looking back and was out into deep water before Janus tapped her on the tail and she swung around to face him.

His arms opened wide as he beheld her. "Princess Kira! Spectacular, even more beautiful than I imagined!"

Kira, in turn, was admiring Janus in all his merman splendor. His long golden hair was still tied behind, but his muscular arms and scale-covered chest were exposed, no longer hidden by a shirt. What surprised her most was the bronze colour of his scales. She had been expecting the blue grey of central Atlantic merrows that Currin had described, though Janus was from Europe, farther east.

"Nice scales," she remarked as they resumed swimming side by side at a leisurely pace. "Are all the Danish merrows bronze like you?"

"Some are. Some are more silver or grey. A bit of blue and green also. I think there are some in-between merrows, perhaps a Spegar father and a mother from around the British Isles or Scandinavia. My parents were different colours, one pinkish grey and one bronze. Are your royal parents the same?"

Kira looked at him, puzzled. "I don't know. Currin was gold, and I think Calista was bronze or silver. I don't remember. I was only a year old when we were separated, and I haven't seen them as merrows since then."

"This must be sad for them?"

"Yes, especially for my father."

"But you call Cillian 'father' also. Is this confusing?"

Kira laughed. "At first, it was a bit awkward because my real parents—I mean, my royal parents—were strangers to me. Five years later, it feels normal to have two fathers and two mothers. I call Currin and Calista by their names, and Cillian and Bess are Dad and Mom. Anyway, I consider myself doubly lucky, especially when I know others who only have one parent or none."

"And your cousins, they live with Currin and Calista. How do they address them?"

"Like me, just by their names, Currin and Calista. Amelie has adapted very well. But I think it has been especially hard for Borin to have lost both his parents." Kira decided to say nothing more about him. Very few merrows knew that Borin's mother was finfolk, and she didn't wish to prejudice Janus against Borin, especially when they were about to go to war against the finfolk.

"Yes," Janus agreed, "but I think Borin should be happy if we can find his parents once we have Merhaven back. They may have been chased out when the finfolk invaded. Or do you think the finfolk have imprisoned them, or something worse?"

Kira was afraid to meet Janus's eyes. She continued to look straight ahead. "I'm not sure what we'll find," she said. "Borin doesn't talk about it, so neither do we. I expect he is prepared for the worst."

"Yes, perhaps so. Look, Kira! A garden of seagrass." Janus pointed to a large undulating mat of tall plants ahead of them. "I hear you are interested in studying sea plants to feed people on land and to develop into medicine."

Kira stopped in the middle of the patch and sank into it. "Do you think that's weird?" She looked up at him as he smiled at her. She stared at his eyes. In this filtered light, definitely dark green, she thought. He drifted down, closer to her face, and then reached out with his hands to touch her cheeks.

"No, Kira, it is not weird. It is very generous of you, most proper for one of royal blood to be thinking of others." He drew her face closer to his and then kissed her on the lips. He let her go immediately and backed up.

"Please forgive me! I do not know what made me do this."

Kira was speechless and disappointed. Her lips still tingled from the fleeting kiss.

"Yes, I will forgive you…but only if you kiss me again," she said, trying to keep a serious expression.

Janus looked surprised. "You are serious?"

She nodded, the corners of her mouth crinkling. He approached her with a wicked smile and kissed her again, a much longer, lingering kiss. When they finally broke apart, Kira smiled up at him. "Much better," she said.

They swam farther, holding hands, saying little. As they emerged from the water, Janus pointed at her Pendright. "That must be a special pendant. It is shaped like the gavel Curtis uses at meetings. Is it a symbol of your clan?"

"Yes, this Pendright is passed along the royal line." Kira clasped it with her free hand and sighed deeply.

"I believe it is where it should be, and you will be a fine leader for your clan," Janus said, squeezing her hand. "Will you return to Merhaven once it is freed of finfolk?"

Kira nearly stopped in her tracks. No one had ever asked her that. She wondered if Janus was merely curious or he expected her to assume the role of merrow queen.

"To be honest, I never really thought about it. I've always planned to go to university, to study marine botany and biochemistry. You know, there is so much we can learn from the sea. I just read an article about a biotech company that studies venom from sea anemones. They use it to treat people with autoimmune diseases, like psoriasis and multiple sclerosis. I think that's amazing!"

Janus stopped walking and looked at her, still holding her hand. "I can see how excited you are about this. This research, it can help people, yes?"

"Yes!"

"But what will it do for your own kind, the merrows? Do they suffer from these same diseases in the sea?"

Kira shook her head. "I don't know. I'd have to find out. That's what researchers do."

"But if you stay on land too long, you will not be able to return to the water to do this research in later years."

"Well, I suppose I'd need to work with merrows to help me get that information."

Janus laughed. "Perhaps if you have their trust. It may not be so easy, though."

Kira frowned. She had no idea how to respond. She didn't like the idea of losing her ability to change into merrow form. She knew she would have to choose land or water eventually, but she didn't want to think about it now.

"What about you, Janus? What are your plans?"

"Call me a freedom fighter if you like. I work for the merrow tribes of the world. If humans are useful, I use them. But they are not my first concern."

They had resumed a slow walk, still hand in hand.

"Your ambitions are noble, Janus. I wish there were more merrows like you."

"We just have to find them, Kira. And we will." He squeezed her hand tightly and flashed her a smile.

For a moment, Kira pictured herself on the throne of Merhaven, with Janus sitting next to her. She wondered what vision might be passing through his mind. Then she blushed and blinked rapidly to clear the thought away. She was content to be walking on the beach with a handsome young merrow, hoping he could not hear her pounding heart. Was this how it felt at the beginning of love? If so, she hoped her heart would be strong enough.

Chapter 6 –
Merrows in Arms

THE PREPARATION FOR Operation Free Merhaven was nothing like the frantic activity before they set sail for Hildaland years before. For one thing, most of the action was beneath the surface of the sea: training volunteers to appear threatening and to defend themselves with spears and monitoring movements of the finfolk. Because the merrows could not morph into camouflaged forms, they depended on dolphins to do surveillance.

Above the surface, most of the preparation took place in Bevanton, where the spears were being made at a metal shop. Currin was most particular with the details. The spear he wanted them to reproduce had an unusual design and metal composition, which sparked a great deal of curiosity amongst the metal workers. Where had it come from? Who had designed it? Why did they use that particular blend of metals? Fred and Currin had concocted a story about finding the spear in the attic of an old house. Then, by accident, they discovered it had excellent properties for spear fishing. They said they planned to sell them out of Currin's shop to divers who enjoyed sport fishing. That, plus the hefty fees for producing the spears, seemed to satisfy the shop manager.

In return for assisting in the upcoming battle, the Spegar hunters had asked for a number of spears to take back to their tribe. Currin and Fred ordered the production of at least the same number to keep for themselves. The thought had occurred to a number of council members that it would be wise to keep spears on hand. They were concerned by the arrival of finfolk and armed merrows in their usually peaceful waters. Kira was relieved to know that she was not the only one with reservations about the Spegar tribe and others like them.

She was also happy to discover that Steen had contacted neighbouring dolphin pods to inform them of the planned merrow offensive against the finfolk in Merhaven. Given the finfolk taste for young dolphins, Steen had no trouble rounding up a good number of mature dolphins who volunteered to keep an eye on the movement of the invaders.

Either Steen or Cass reported to Kira every other day in the two weeks before the operation was to start. "We found eight underground entrances to Merhaven so far," Cass told her, trembling with excitement. "They carry things away, and bring other things in, like food, lots of it. They love small squid and octopuses and fish. We think eels are their favourite food, even the electric ones. Buzz!" He vibrated his entire body, something Kira had never seen him do before. Then he broke into convulsive laughter.

"Cass, you're such a comedian. But seriously, could you see what they were taking away?" Kira asked.

"Not really. Square things, round things, long things. Some are white. Some are gold."

"Oh dear. I'll bet they're looting the palace. Maybe they know we're coming after them."

"You know, Princess, they love metal, so they will take it all away if they can."

Kira nodded. "Yes, I know. We have the spears now, and if our warriors-in-training are ready soon enough, I think we may want to move in earlier."

"You will let us know?" Cass seemed worried. He was not the totally carefree youngster he once was.

"Yes, of course! I'll send the signal we agreed on. Early morning in the next few days, right?"

"We're always tuned in, Princess!" Cass waved a flipper as he swam off.

Kira decided it was time for that talk with Currin. Once she was back at home, she called him at work. She asked if they could meet at his office when he was done for the day. He told her to come right over.

He led her to his small office at the back of the fish plant. The room was infused with the smell of brewed coffee. Currin had become a connoisseur of freshly ground, organically grown coffee, and he offered Kira a cup. She declined. She was agitated enough and afraid caffeine would make her airborne.

"You have a dolphin report for us?" Currin guessed.

"Yes, and it's not good news. Finfolk have been carrying a lot of stuff out of Merhaven lately. I think they might be emptying it."

Currin nodded. "I am sure they are pillaging the palace. That is what they do, scavenge for any piece of metal, precious or not. Anything useful. They might even be dismantling the palace, stone by stone from the inside out. They do not care for art. They have no sense of beauty."

"Do you think they know we're coming?"

"They may not be certain, but they are always ready to defend themselves. We are the ones who must be fully prepared before we attack."

"I know, Currin, but I have a bad feeling that things may not go according to our plan. That we should be more careful about who knows all the details." Kira paused and took a deep breath. "These Spegar merrows, for instance. I don't trust them completely. They're like mercenaries."

"Right now, we can use any allies willing to help, Kira, including mercenaries. But I understand your discomfort. And remember, we will now have our own weapons once they have gone back home."

"*If* they go home," Kira grumbled. She took another deep breath. "And what about Borin? His mother is probably in the palace. Wouldn't it be best if he didn't participate in the attack? Isn't that a conflict of interest?"

"Borin is completely on our side. He has proved his loyalty over and over, Kira."

"But what if he comes face to face with her or with his father? He might not even know what his reaction will be. Other merrows might get hurt if he hesitates or does the wrong thing. Or *he* might get hurt."

"Kira, you are worried about something that will likely not happen. Anyway, you know that the orders are to chase them off, not to hurt or kill them. If Nim is still at the palace, that is another matter. He is a traitor, and the council will need to decide how to deal with him. Borin would be excused from participating in that process."

"Okay, but I think we should move as soon as we're ready, not the day we were planning on. Even a day or two earlier, so if the finfolk are suspicious, we have a chance to surprise them."

"Ha, you have become quite the strategist, Kira!"

She stood up and began to pace, her fists clenched. "I also think that the Spegar hunters should not know if we change the day. Only the group captains should be informed, and only at the last minute."

Currin studied his daughter: her determined expression, her spear straight back, her suppression of her own desire to join the attack in deference to all four of her parents.

"I will talk this over with Curtis and Fred. The element of surprise is a good strategy, I know. Your mother and I were once the victims of such a surprise. Keeping it secret will be the hardest part. We shall see what we can do."

"Now I have a proposal for you, Kira. I would like to send you as an emissary to each of the battle squads. I would ask you to deliver, on behalf of the royal family, a message of encouragement and appreciation to the troops. And I think I know how we can prime them for an early surprise attack without them knowing it." Kira and Currin spent the rest of the evening preparing for her next move.

They were five days out from the proposed battle day when Kira set out the following morning to visit each group. She had learned exactly where the merrow squads were located and their training timetables so she could avoid the Spegar trainers. After delivering the message from Currin, she had a private meeting with each captain to assess each squad's readiness for battle. She also advised the captains that they would be alerted by special messenger if there were any change in the time of assembly and initiation of Operation Free Merhaven. Finally, she presented each captain with a gold-coloured belt adorned with the symbol of Atlanta Maris, which was to be worn from that day until the end of the operation.

Shortly after noon, Kira had one near encounter with the Spegar hunters. She spotted them in the distance, pursued by one of the local squads on a training exercise. Once again, she wished her scales could be dulled to blend in with the rocky bottom. She escaped detection by diving into a thick bed of kelp. Kira caught a fleeting glimpse of Janus, his bronze scales distinct among the grey and silver of the others. She felt a twinge of guilt at deceiving him. He was devoting his time and energy to helping her merrow community take back their territory, and she was sneaking around behind his back.

When her squad visits were completed, and all the captains' belts delivered and secured around their waists, she swam in search of

Steen's pod. The dolphins' cooperation was also vital to the timing of an early attack.

By the end of the day, Kira was truly exhausted. No amount of coffee would keep her awake that night. She had one more phone call to make before she could tumble into bed.

"Currin here. What's the news?"

Kira found herself gripping the phone like it might fly away. "They're ready. All of them. And the messengers are on board. What's your news?"

She heard Currin expel his breath before he spoke. "Care to go fishing tomorrow?"

"Sure. See you dark and early."

* * *

IN THE CHILL BLACK of pre-dawn, the Cox household was awake as usual. What was not normal was how Bess and Kira were dressed, ready to board Cillian's fishing boat for a day out on the water. Both of them had called in sick, trying to speak with convincingly raspy voices. Bess was especially nervous and nearly broke into a fit of giggles. They made their way to the wharf amidst the crowd of village fishers heading off for a regular day of deep-sea fishing. Kira and Bess, with their caps pulled low over their heads and with their hair tucked into their jackets, hurried down into the hold of the boat to escape recognition. Fred had already sent his fishing crew off without him, telling them he was spending the day on Cillian's boat. As they pushed off from the wharf, Kira spied a groggy Borin shuffling behind Currin. The entire scene was in such stark contrast to the open excitement of the morning they had set out to storm Hildaland. Very few people awake at that hour had any idea of the storm brewing below the calm surface of the water.

Once they were well out of the harbour, Kira removed her outer gear and boots, gave her mother a hug, and then slipped over the side of the boat. She swam quickly to a point that opened into the larger bay and settled herself on the silted bottom behind a rock outcrop. She used both hands to dig furiously in the sand, stirring it up until she found herself in a cloud of agitated particles. As they drifted back down around her, she was holding a spear in her hands, the one she had planted there two days earlier. *Now* she was ready.

"*EE-U-EE-U-EE!*" she broadcast her call into the dark water and then leaned back against the rough rock to wait. Around her, the water pulsed with life. Tiny fingerlings flitted past, and larger fish cruised by slowly. Sea fronds waved gently in the current, growing lighter and greener as the reluctant sun crept higher in the sky. A smattering of clicks caught Kira's attention, and she scanned the distant water. Two black points soon turned into approaching dolphins. Waiting until she was certain, Kira poked her hand out as Rom and Tork rounded the corner. They both reared up in alarm, and she dropped the spear.

"Sorry—I didn't mean to scare you."

"Just surprised," Rom said, wiggling. "I never saw one of those close up. The finfolk are in big trouble now!" Both dolphins laughed. Rom added, "The messengers have been sent out."

"Excellent!" Kira rubbed her hands together and then picked up her spear.

"Will you come with us?" Tork asked. "We can escort you to your boat."

"You don't need to do that." Kira did not wish to draw them any nearer to danger. Once the finfolk were all out of the palace and in open water, there was no telling what could happen.

"Yes, we must. We have our orders from Steen. And we are faster than finfolk. There's no need to worry about us," Rom said. Kira noticed a small dolphin smile.

"Okay then, let's go!"

She had decided not to return to the boat. Kira had not seen Merhaven in over five years. It was a long swim, but she preferred that to pacing the small deck of Cillian's boat and gnawing her nails for three hours, nails that were already chewed as far as possible without ripping into her fingertips. Her parents would be displeased, but she could not share her plan earlier because they would protest and fret needlessly. Kira could not possibly stay up top, not knowing what was happening below. Merrows who had pledged allegiance to her family were fighting for her ancestral home.

Kira figured they were not far behind the boats on their way to Merhaven, and once she spotted Cillian's vessel above, she asked Rom to deliver a message to her mother. "Tell Bess that I am swimming to the palace with a dolphin escort and I promise to stay out of trouble. Tell her I have a spear and I know how to use it." She could already picture the apoplectic expression on her mother's face when she heard the message. "Sorry, Mom," she murmured as Rom sped away and up to the boat.

He was back within a minute. "She was not pleased. She said, 'Enjoy the swim.'" Then he quivered with amusement.

They passed all the boats in the next half-hour. Shortly after they lost sight of the last one, Kira saw her first armed merrows. At first glance, she wondered if they might be Spegar hunters. However, as they swam closer, she realized they were some of the locals she had visited the other day. Four, five, six merrows, she mentally counted. All raised their spears in salute when they recognized her; their surprised expressions quickly replaced with smiles and welcoming nods.

Their captain, his long white hair flowing behind him, swam up next to her, although Rom and Tork did not budge from her sides.

"Princess Kira, you are joining us today?"

"Yes, I am, Elder Crane. I'll try to stay out of the way so I don't cause you any concern. But I've been practising with the spear underwater. I used to throw the javelin on land, which is not the same I know, and I don't plan to throw this one. I am comfortable holding and using it if necessary, though."

"I am pleased to see you here. Your presence will be appreciated by the troops. Your bravery on land and in the sea sets a fine example for our merrowlings. We are all proud to serve you and your family." He bowed his head and swam back to his squad. His words bolstered Kira's confidence and resolve that she had made the right decision. Elder Crane had been appointed lead captain of the operation, with seven sub-captains under his command.

In the meantime, Kira noticed another squad of merrows had swum in from a different sector. Their captain also raised his spear to her when she acknowledged him with a nod. As her heart swelled with pride, she felt so humbled to witness all these merrows gathering at the behest of her family and the Merrowmind Council. She wished Currin could have been here, leading his tribes into battle.

Just then, Borin swam into view. When he saw Kira, his brow furrowed and he swam directly into her path, forcing her to stop. "So, what's this? Are you taking over now?" His lips pressed together as if an invisible hand had clamped them shut.

"Don't worry, Borin. I'm only a figurehead. I'll stay out of your way. There's no change in plans."

"Only a major time change, which I'm sure you had something to do with."

"It was the king's decision to make, not mine. I'm not here to interfere."

"No? So, where's Janus? Where are the Spegars, our best fighters? Did anyone bother to tell them we moved up the day?"

"Borin, you aren't listening! These aren't my decisions to make. Take this up with the king! And get of our way. You're holding us up!" Kira shot up over top of Borin, the two dolphins sticking to her like synchronized swimmers.

She was glad that Elder Crane's squad was far enough ahead to miss that exchange. However, she was sure that a few nearby merrows did witness the royal row. It was poor timing on Borin's part. With all the anger boiling up and out of him, Kira hoped he wouldn't do anything rash. She wondered now if she should have stayed on the boat after all. She began to question her motivation for coming. Maybe it had something to do with showing up her hotheaded, resentful cousin.

Well, perhaps it was a little, but a larger part was the sense of duty to her heritage, to her parents, and to the merrows who wished to live in peace and safety after losing their king and queen. She was the face of the royal line, the bearer of the Pendright. She belonged to them. She was one of them. Borin was not, though he'd been raised to believe he was.

Kira shrugged and refocused on what was ahead. She had to pay attention, be aware of anything unusual, such as floating logs and clumps of weeds that could morph back into finfolk torpedoes in a millisecond. She had lived through such an experience once and vowed it would never happen to her again. She also felt responsible for the dolphins next to her. She wished she could send them back to safety, but they were as loyal to her as they were to their own pod. Plus, they provided her with two more sets of eyes and excellent senses; they would keep each other safer in a mini pod of dolphins and merrow.

They still had a long swim ahead, possibly two more hours, Kira figured, though human land time was hard to gauge underwater. Gradually, she recognized features of the seabed, landmarks that let her know they were approaching Merhaven. She noticed that the squads of merrows had split up and fanned out so that they would be approaching the palace from all directions. Designated merrows would enter the escape tunnels to flush any finfolk back into the palace, where they would have to exit. This was to ensure that all their enemies had left and none were still lurking in tunnels. Afterwards, the tunnel exits would be guarded and then sealed.

Kira suddenly realized that they were alone, she and her dolphin escorts. "Rom, Tork, you know what to look for."

"Yes," they both answered. They had been using their natural sonar to detect anything moving around them.

"Only fish so far," Rom said. "Nothing larger on the move."

Kira flipped herself as she swam so she was staring up at the surface about thirty dolphin lengths above. There was nothing to see except the blue of the sky on a clear, sunny summer day. She flipped over again when Rom squeaked, "Look to the right and up!"

Kira's jaw dropped. A shark! A large one zeroing in on them. She lifted her spear, grabbing it with both hands, and steeled herself for impact. The two dolphins had left her sides and were zigzagging crazily in front of the shark. The large predator slowed and turned his attention on Tork. Rom, who had swum around the back, rammed the shark's side and then flipped off quickly to stay out of reach. Kira, terrified that the shark might grab one of them, swam straight toward the beast as he swung his head back in Tork's direction again. He turned his head toward her just as she jabbed the spear up into his nose. The shark reared up, with Kira hanging onto the spear as she was tossed over his head. She didn't dare let go, she thought, or she'd have nothing to protect them. She beat her tail hard and found herself near the surface, spear in hand and detached from the shark. Where was he?

She looked around, then above, and, finally, below, where she saw a plume of blood suspended in the water. There were no dolphins or a shark to be seen. Where were they? Near the surface, she swung around and around, searching below, but there was nothing to see. She was alone.

"EE-U!" she whistled. It wasn't a distress call; however, if her friends were near, they would know to be careful and that she was okay. She swam away from the plume, still constantly scanning for signs of life. She believed the shark would not be coming back for her, but she desperately hoped the dolphins had gotten away from him. Or was it a morphed finfolk? Sharks were not common in this area, though they showed up from time to time. She recalled the shark sentries around Hildaland. Of course, where there were finfolk, there were often large sharks. Ugh.

She heard a series of clicks and smiled. Three dolphins swam toward her, Cass in the lead, followed by his pals, Rom and Tork.

"You're okay!" she called out to them raising her spear.

"Better than okay!" Rom shouted. "That big boy won't be coming back soon." He bounced up and down in the water with glee.

"We ran into our sentry pod," Tork said. "The rest are chasing the shark to make sure he keeps going. But with all the blood trailing him, they'll turn back soon."

Cass nodded at Kira. "I hear you have good aim, Princess. Congratulations. And thank you for protecting my friends."

"Oh no, they were protecting me. We're a team. Right, guys? He didn't morph into a finfolk, did he?"

"No, that was a shark," Cass confirmed. "A very big shark."

"Okay, now I'm really worried about the operation at Merhaven. They might have more of these big guys around. I need to keep moving. I don't think we're far now. But you should not come closer. You've done enough for us."

Cass swam up to Kira's face, beak to nose, and said, "You think we're going to leave now? You know me better than that!" He turned away and began to swim. "What are you waiting for? Let's go!"

The four of them continued toward Merhaven, with Cass in the lead, Kira right behind, and Rom and Tork on either side, slightly above and behind her. They swam in tight formation, without incident, until the appearance of a faint white glow in the distance: Merhaven, at last.

Chapter 7 -
Operation Free Merhaven

KIRA FOUND HERSELF tightening the grip on her spear. They had slowed and lowered themselves so they were skimming the sea bottom, still scanning the water around them. The palace was a huge structure, covering the same area as a football field on land. She could see merrows hovering around the entire structure at equal intervals, like a crocheted blanket draped over it. Nothing seemed to be happening. She signalled for her three companions to stop and wait.

The palace gates and doors were shut tight. There was no movement anywhere nearby, except for the armed merrows and occasional fish. Kira stared at the rocks and seaweed beds suspiciously, wondering if they might suddenly come to life and release finfolk. However, all looked normal and peaceful, as if Merhaven were abandoned or completely asleep.

Elder Crane and four other merrows swam up to the main doors and attempted to pull them open, but they did not budge. They rapped the butts of their spears on the doors. "Open the doors at once in the name of King Currin Corinalis of Atlanta Maris, sovereign of Oceana!" Elder Crane's deep voice created a sonic boom underwater. Kelp fronds bent over as the vibration passed through them. Still, the doors did not open. On a signal, the enclosing net of merrows began pounding their spears on the sides and roof of the palace, including the clear crystal ceiling over the gardens at the rear of the building.

Suddenly the main doors flew open, and a dozen finfolk vaulted out at once. Elder Crane's group moved back to let them pass as the finfolk lashed out with their claws, snapping their sharp metallic teeth in human-like faces. Except for the teeth and the spiked fin protruding from the top of their heads, they could be mistaken for dark-coloured merrows at a distance.

The merrows held out their spears to keep the finfolk away, but there was no attempt on either side to engage in combat. Kira noticed that Borin had joined the merrows by the main doors, watching intently as more finfolk streamed past.

Kira kept her spear pointed in front of her while Rom kept watch behind as the finfolk swam by them and away from Merhaven. He continually reported what he saw to let them know none of the enemy was returning to attack their backs. Meanwhile, the number of finfolk exiting the palace had decreased, until there was nothing for quite some time.

Two other captains had joined Elder Crane at the entrance, and they finally entered the palace, about twenty-five armed merrows in all. Kira assumed Borin was with them. He knew the interior of the palace well, his old home. He'd be able to check all the rooms to make sure it was empty of finfolk. Another dozen merrows remained at the entrance to guard it.

"Incoming log, up top! Make that three logs!" Rom shouted. Kira whirled around.

"Finfolk attacking!" Kira yelled. She rose slightly, her spear raised in front of her. The disguised finfolk had speed and weight on their side, and when Kira's spear made contact, the butt rammed into her Pendright, driving her back into the ground. Kira was face to face with a screaming, gnashing mouthful of teeth, claws raking her arms. She pushed the spear away with all her strength into a roiling mass of bodies and turbulence. As the pressure on her chest was relieved, she wondered that she felt no pain from the impact, only a gentle radiating warmth.

The water around her was murky. The finfolk seemed to be gone, and only Cass remained, staring at her. "You're hurt. You're bleeding," he said.

Kira looked down at herself. Her arms were scratched but hardly bleeding.

"That's not my blood," she said, realizing why the water around her had become so dingy.

"Princess Kira!" One of the merrows swam up to her.

"I'm fine!" she said before he could ask. "What happened to those finfolk?"

He pointed away from the palace. "We chased them off. The dolphins knocked two of them away, and you skewered one of them. That's his blood, I guess." He frowned when he pointed at the cloudy water, slowly clearing. "I hear finfolk blood can be toxic. We should move away from it."

She turned back to Cass as they swam. "Where are Rom and Tork? Are they okay?"

He tilted his head. "Not sure. I need to check."

"Go ahead, Cass. I'll be safe here with these fine fellows. Go on, and let me know how they are. And please be careful."

Cass disappeared in an instant. Kira knew he was worried...as was she.

"Can we go inside now? Has anyone given the all-clear yet?" she asked the merrow who was obviously not going to leave her side. Two other merrows had joined them, and one said he'd heard the palace was now free of finfolk.

At the entrance, the guards saluted Kira and waved her inside without exchanging a word. This was an instance when she didn't mind being singled out by her scale colouring and the brilliant Pendright. In these circumstances, she supposed, it could be taken for a piece of armour, a metal breastplate.

Once inside, she was again awed by the brilliance of the white pillars and the immensity of the place. Though she had only been there once, she remembered that the walls had a gold sheen then. Now they were a dull grey, as if the gold had become tarnished or had peeled off. And the curtains of pink seagrass were gone, exposing all the rooms they had once covered. Except for the odd shelf, the rooms were completely empty.

Looking ahead, she could see into the throne room, now filled with merrows swimming back and forth. Two tall golden doors used to open into that room. They had vanished. The finfolk had looted the palace and removed all the metal ornaments, fixtures, and furniture. As she passed into the throne room, she noticed the floor, once lined with pink and gold tiles in the shape of starfish, was now the grey and black of the rock subsurface. The thrones had also been removed, which did not sadden Kira, for the memory of Shree and Nim sitting on them made her stomach turn.

Elder Crane swam up to Kira and nodded. "I am afraid it is the disaster we thought it would be. But at least they are gone, except for a handful of merrows who remained behind with Nim."

"Nim is still here?" Kira was surprised. She thought he might have wanted to leave. "And what about Shree? Gone, I suppose?"

"No sign of her, Princess Kira. Borin is with them now, speaking with Nim. I presume he would have recognized Shree if she were still in her merrow form."

Kira did not answer. She had no idea if one finfolk could morph into different merrow forms. She assumed all the remaining merrows would be suspects until they were exposed to the air at the surface, when their true identities could be confirmed.

"Princess Kira, I hear you had a brief encounter with a finfolk.

Do you require medical attention?" he asked, looking at her raked arms.

"Oh no, I'm fine, really. Just scratches. I think the finfolk that impaled himself on my spear got the worst of it." She had to smile a little, as gruesome as the image was.

"Would you care to join Borin with the Merhaven merrows? They are being questioned by Captain Mak."

Kira was torn. She wanted to see who was left behind, but she didn't want to deal with Borin.

"I would like to see them, but not Nim if Borin is talking to him now, if that is possible."

Elder Crane nodded and left. He returned shortly and asked her to follow him. They swam through a series of corridors, reminding Kira of how easy it was to get lost in the palace. A kind elderly servant had shown her the way out when she decided to escape several years ago.

Elder Crane told Kira that the merrows had been found huddled in one of the back rooms off the kitchen. They were taken to the garden at the back where there was more light, the place where Kira had played hide-and-seek with Borin and Amelie when she first met them. As they entered the play area, Kira felt her heart constrict. The play domes had been totally dismantled, with smashed crystal tiles strewn about. The small garden plots were overgrown with weeds, and the filthy floor was littered with decayed food and rubble.

The merrows lay on the ground or sat on what clean surfaces remained. At first glance, they appeared exhausted and ill. Their skin was sallow; their scales, the colour of lead; and their hair, stringy. Most of them were elderly, with greying or white hair. Kira examined their faces carefully. None looked anything like Shree. They all had large merrow eyes, mostly blue, green, or light brown. They did not have the darting black minnow eyes of the finfolk queen. Kira could feel the muscles in her neck and back relaxing, though her scraped arm was beginning to throb. Then she recognized one of them.

Kira swam toward the old woman with a downcast face. The elderly mermaid squinted at Kira, and her mouth began to tremble. "It is the princess herself! You have returned for us! Thanks be to Neptune!" She raised up her thin arms, and Kira took her pale, wrinkled hands in her own.

"And I thank you for helping me escape this place all those years ago. Do you remember? I am sorry I took so long to return."

The old maid was shaking, so Kira sat next to her and put her arm around her bony old shoulders. The others also looked like they could use a long rest and some nourishing food. Once again, Kira felt herself simmering at the thought of the abuse they had suffered. It did not appear that any of the merrows had remained in Merhaven of their own free will once the finfolk took over.

Captain Mak said, "We will take them back with us and care for them, Princess. Food will be arriving shortly." His face was grim, and Kira could see he was struggling not to voice his thoughts. She gave him an understanding nod. She could barely hold back her own tears.

When Nim entered the old garden, Kira did not recognize him at first. He had aged twenty years over the last five. Apparently, he had not been treated well, either. She had always thought of him as weak-willed and not very bright. However, right then, she understood that he was also a victim, manipulated by a powerful sorceress. She hoped Borin had not been too hard on him.

Nim did not look at anyone in the room. He drifted down to the ground and sat there, as dejected as the rest. He had fallen farther and harder than any of them.

When food had arrived, Kira ate a little with the freed merrows and some of the rescue squad. She chatted with them, trying to remain positive for their sakes. She hadn't realized how hungry or tired she was herself. And she wasn't surprised when a messenger arrived to tell her there was a boat waiting for her on the surface, with an anxious king aboard. Kira wished them all well and promised to look in on them once they had resettled in new homes. It was obvious the palace was not fit for anyone to live in, even if had they wanted to stay.

Elder Crane escorted Kira to the surface. He explained to her that he had already given the first status report of the operation to Currin, who could fill her in on details. He was also anxious to return home, but not before the palace was secure and a constant guard arranged.

As they broke through to the surface, Kira heard a strange sound over the noise of running engines and slapping waves, like a disordered series of dolphin clicks. When she looked up at the boats, everyone was clapping.

"Hooray for our warrior princess!" She discerned the unmistakable voice of Curtis shouting from his boat and several cheers from the other boats gathered around.

Currin leaned over the side of his vessel, holding out a hand to haul Kira on board. As she flipped into the boat and transformed back into human form, she caught the look in Currin's eyes—pain mixed with envy.

"Thank you, Elder Crane," he said. "We are forever grateful to you and all the merrows who liberated Merhaven."

The older merrow nodded, saluted, and disappeared into the sea.

"So, no spear?" Currin laughed. "I am glad you did not bring it up with you. I hear you have excellent aim."

Kira nodded, grinning. She was still sprawled on the deck, sopping wet and starting to feel chilled in the east evening wind. She didn't know if she could stand up.

"You had better wave at Cillian and Bess over there to let them know you survived. I will get you a blanket. A change of dry clothes for you is on their boat." Kira hauled herself up and located Cillian's boat. Without her glasses, she had to go by the colour patterns to identify it. She whistled at them and waved. Their boat moved closer so they could talk. Currin had returned from below and draped a thick, warm blanket around her shoulders, covering up her scraped arms. Out of the water, she had noticed that the scratches had become angry red welts. Nurse Bess would be all over her, back at home.

"How are you?" Bess shouted.

"I'm fine, Mom. Sorry I didn't tell you, I—"

"Never mind, it's okay. As long as you came back in one piece. Honestly, Kira, I—"

"We're proud of you, Kira!" Cillian interrupted. "See you at home!"

Then the tears came. She turned away from her parents' boat so they wouldn't see her cry. And there was Borin on the deck, dripping wet and staring at her with a blank expression. Was he going to laugh at her now? Kira tried to suck back her tears and hiccupped.

"Feeling a little emotional just now," she said, "after seeing those merrows."

Borin turned his stare to the deck in front of his feet. "Yeah, it was pretty bad."

Kira hiccupped again but didn't speak.

"I saw my father," he said.

"Mm-hmm. He didn't look well, either."

"No. He could hardly say a word. No excuses, no explanations. There's nothing left of him, just a shell."

Kira waited, not knowing if he expected her to say anything. She hiccupped again.

"He was a good father when we were young. He did his best. Those creatures are evil. They're monsters!"

Kira nodded. "Yeah, they are. I'm sorry, Borin," she whispered, and the deluge began anew. She closed her eyes and sobbed uncontrollably. Moments later, she opened her eyes in disbelief and then widened them in wonder: Borin was holding her, his body shuddering against hers. She slipped her own arms around his waist, and they mourned together.

Chapter 8 –
After Freedom

BESS PUT ON HER NURSE'S CAP to tend to the ugly scratches on Kira's arms as predicted. Once she was out of the water and dry, her arms felt like they were on fire. What surprised Kira most was the treatment. By the time she walked in the door of her home, Bess already had long brown strips of dried seaweed soaking in a basin of water. They resembled dirty strands of rope as they began to swell. "Go take a shower, Kira. When you're towelled off, give me a shout," her mother instructed.

When she was much younger, Kira remembered that her scraped knees and elbows were treated with pale-green or -pink gels. Bess had concocted these remedies herself, but Kira never questioned what they were. She rarely sported a bandage like her schoolmates did. Her wounds healed quickly, and she never gave it another thought.

"What kind of seaweed is this, Mom?" She watched as Bess squeezed out the excess water and then gently placed a slimy brown strand over each scratch.

"We merrows call it finfix. I don't actually know the official Latin name for the seaweed. You'll have to tell me once you've studied all the sea plants at university."

"There's a book on northern Atlantic seaweeds at the library. I can look it up tomorrow. Maybe you can draw a picture of a live plant for me so that I'll know what to look for. And tell me where you found it."

Bess shook her head. "Calista gave it to me, actually. The merrow fishers get it caught on their lines sometimes, and they know it has medicinal properties, so they save it for us."

"That's awesome, Mom!" Kira raised an arm to give it a pump and then winced.

"You'll be sore for a day or two. This stuff isn't magic, you know. But it works much better than anything you'll find in a pharmacy. Nothing else heals finfolk wounds without leaving scars."

Kira pondered that for a moment. She had actually been looking forward to having scars on her arms, a sort of validation of the Pendright she wore. Not as neat and pretty as the tattoos so many people liked to show off, but they were honestly acquired. Of course, such scars could not be explained to people who were unaware of the existence of merrows and finfolk. As she left the bathroom to get dressed, she thought she might remove the finfix once the swelling had subsided but before she was fully healed, leaving a wee hint of her battle scars.

A cartoon bubble image suddenly popped into her head. She was showing off her injuries to Janus. His hands were on his hips, a scowl on his face. How was she going to explain leaving him out of the battle? Would he be angry with her? Would he leave right away because Merhaven had been freed and the operation was over? She should call him and explain…unless he already knew.

"Hi, it's Kira here," she spoke into the phone.

"Kira!" Amelie squealed. "I heard you got hurt, and you nailed one of those horrible finfolk. Are you okay?"

Kira moved the phone back to her ear. "I'm fine, Amelie. I just have some scratches. I'm wondering if Currin is there and if he has time to talk with me."

"Oh, sure. Fred's here with him, but he can talk. Uncle Currin, it's Kira!"

Kira shook her head but had to smile at Amelie's explosive energy. She hadn't wanted to interrupt Currin if he had company.

"Kira, dear, how are you now?"

"Mom—um, Bess fixed me up. I'll be okay. I just wondered if anyone called Janus to let him know. I still feel bad, cutting him out of the whole thing."

"It has been taken care of. Curtis called from his boat on the way back home. Janus was, of course, disappointed, but he understands. He is a sensible young man. He thinks the Spegars will not be pleased, but they trained our merrows as we had asked them to do, and we will pay them as we had agreed. We should have the last of their spears ready in two or three days."

"Oh, good. Who's going to hand the spears over to them?"

"Fred and I were just discussing that. I think the same three mermen who found our squads of volunteer warriors and Elder Crane if he is willing." Currin paused a moment. "Do you want to join them, Kira?"

Kira hesitated, suddenly uncertain what she wanted to say. "Borin. How is he?"

"He is recovering. He is in shock, Kira. Seeing his father that way... well, he was not prepared for it."

"I know. And he still wants to deliver the spears?"

"Yes, I believe he does. He is determined to see this through to the end."

Kira imagined what that would be like, with Borin and Janus and Chris. They would be carrying twenty spears to the Spegars. With herself and Elder Crane along, there would be five merrows. She realized she still didn't trust the green merrows. However, if there were trouble, the odds would be about even with her along. "Yes, I'd like to go. I'll be fine by then."

"Very well. I'll let you know when the spears are ready."

***

THREE DAYS LATER, Curtis's and Currin's boats left the wharf along with Fred, Cillian, the four young merrows, and twenty-four spears. They were heading for a rendezvous point halfway to Merhaven. On board, Janus updated the others on conversations he'd had with the Spegars after they learned that the recapture of Merhaven had proceeded without them.

"They were displeased. I think they might have enjoyed killing a few finfolk."

Currin grunted at that. "Just as well they were not along, then."

"They also wanted to know what was found at Merhaven. I think they did not believe that all the gold and valuable items were gone. Perhaps you could show them?" He looked at Currin.

Currin pulled at his beard, straightening the curls. He smiled wryly. "Now why are they so interested in the gold? Do you suppose they are more than simple fishers?"

"They have no business with Merhaven," Borin said. "They don't need to see it."

"I agree," Kira said, "but what if they won't leave until they do see it for themselves? If they are treasure hunters, they need to know there are no treasures left. They should see the mess left behind."

"What do you think, Janus?" Currin asked.

"They are too curious, I think. Perhaps it would be a good idea to give one of them a tour."

Kira studied Janus's expression, trying to pick up any sign that he was resentful. That morning, the others were joking with Kira about a nickname for her: Princess Lance-a-Lot. Janus had smiled and greeted her in a friendly way when he first saw her, but there was no hint of the warmth he had shown her the last time they'd met. She tried to convince herself that he was simply being discreet. She'd ask to meet with him alone after they had delivered the spears.

By the time they reached the rendezvous area and the four merrows were ready to go into the water, they had still not decided if they would allow the Spegars to enter the palace. No one could prevent them from swimming to Merhaven, of course. However, it was under constant guard, and they would not be allowed inside without permission from Currin.

Once the four were in the water, Fred passed four spears down to them. They would go to their rendezvous location and meet with the Spegars before bringing them up to the boat to receive the spears directly from Currin and Fred.

Borin led the way. They swam a short distance from the boats to a chain of underwater hillocks, where they settled on the bottom to wait. As they scanned the water, Chris asked, "Do you think Elder Crane will come?"

Kira shook her head. "He wasn't too keen on giving the hunters any spears. After what they said about the gold, I also wish we hadn't agreed to do it."

"But without their spears, we wouldn't have been able to get rid of the finfolk," Chris pointed out.

"We would have thought of something," Borin grumbled. "I'm sure we could have designed a spear without theirs or used other weapons. They just happened to show up at the right time. Maybe it wasn't such a coincidence."

"Look! Three merrows," Janus said.

As they swam closer, the white-haired leader became recognizable. He was accompanied by two others from his clan; all three were armed with spears. Elder Crane boomed at them as he neared, "We've seen them! Maybe fifteen Spegars, half of them carrying weapons. Coming this way, not far behind. You should return to your boats!"

"And leave you here?" Borin shouted back.

"No, we will lead them to Merhaven, where we have at least twenty sentries. You need to leave now!"

"You can't outswim them," Chris protested.

"Too late," said Janus, holding his spear in front of him. "Here they are."

They all turned to watch as the figures approached. Kira counted, fourteen in all. They were outnumbered two to one. Maybe the Spegars were not planning an aggressive encounter and were just bringing along reinforcements to help carry all the spears back to Iceland or wherever they came from. Or maybe this was the first wave of an invasion.

Their leader, the one who had spoken to Kira a few weeks ago, now addressed Janus, his words as unintelligible and harsh sounding as before. And he still looked angry. Janus replied slowly, calmly. The Spegar leader pointed to Kira with his spear. She wished she could understand.

Janus shook his head and replied again.

"What are they saying, Janus?" Borin asked.

"They want the spears that were promised, and they want Kira to take them to the palace," he said. "I told them the spears were on the boats and we need to go there. He is not happy with this proposal."

The leader began shouting at Janus, and Elder Crane moved forward. "Janus, tell them to follow us back to the boats." He began to swim away and motioned at the others to come with him. Before he beat his tail a second time, the Spegar leader broke away and stabbed the older merrow in his back, withdrawing his spear as blood gushed out of the deep wound.

"No!" Kira screamed. She launched herself at Elder Crane, who twisted in place and began to drift down to the bottom.

The other merrows held up their spears and charged the Spegars.

"Kira, swim to the boat. They want you!" Janus shouted before he joined the fray.

She was reaching for Elder Crane when the spear was ripped from her grasp. Two Spegars had gripped her arms and begun to pull her away. For a moment, she glimpsed the clash between merrows and Spegars, a mash of bodies and thrusting spears.

"Stop! Let me go!" she cried.

She was wedged in so tightly that she could no longer turn her head to look. Behind her, she imagined the slaughter, the water darkening with the blood of her merrow kin and clan. A roar of fury erupted from deep inside Kira. Anguish and frustration flooded her brain, followed by an explosion of light, and then darkness and silence.

Chapter 9 –
Crystal Clear

SOMETHING WAS KNOCKING on her head, trying to get inside. How could that be? Where was she? Kira's head seared with pain of an intensity she had never known before. She opened her eyes only a crack, for they wouldn't open any more. All was black. Her heart pounded. Was she blind? She was lying on a hard, wet surface, and the arm underneath her body had gone numb. She raised her other hand to her face and stared at her fingers. Gradually, her eyes opened wider, and she could just make out the shape of her hand in the dark. She wasn't blind after all but rather found herself in a lightless chamber.

Beyond her pounding head, she could make out other noises: a hum that she could feel more than hear, occasional faint thuds, and high-pitched squeals. She tried to sit up but began to retch as soon as she moved her head. There was nothing in her stomach, only dry heaves. She put her arm under her head and remained prone on the floor. Then her last memory flashed in front of her eyes. She clamped them shut, but the vision of Elder Crane bleeding would not evaporate. She began to cry but stopped within seconds because of the stabbing pain in her head.

I am alive, she thought. That's good, isn't it? But why am I alive? What do they want? Maybe a ransom? Ha, that won't work. My family isn't wealthy. Why am I here? She drifted into blackness again.

The sharp screech of a door opening woke her. Kira pretended to be asleep, but she knew that one or two people had entered the chamber. She opened an eye a sliver, just enough to make out familiar but unexpected footwear: steel-toed fishing boots.

"She still out, eh?" a deep, gravelly voice spoke.

"Mebbe. Give 'er a poke."

Kira steeled herself for a kick but only felt her foot nudged. She remained still.

"She don't look dangerous," the second man said.

"Hmph! Don't touch that thing 'round her neck. Electric or somethin', burnt my hand. Stupid, cheap jool'ry these kids wear."

"Never mind. The fee's good. Don't know why they want her. Prob'ly has rich folks. Let's go."

As the door creaked closed again, she heard the first man say, "We better come back in an hour. She won't be worth much dead."

Kira let out her breath in relief. When she took in a deep breath, she knew for certain that she was on a fishing boat. The two men had a slight accent—from the US, she thought, maybe Maine or farther south.

The Spegars must have been after her all along. She was thankful she had covered her Pendright when she first ran into them. However, if they had recognized and taken her then, it would have prevented the battle and saved the lives of her friends. In the end, they captured her anyway. She drew in a sharp breath and felt the burn of tears behind her eyes. Her head still throbbed, though the pain had dulled somewhat. Kira put her hand on the Pendright and felt its warmth. It was warmer than her body, but not hot. She noticed that her head no longer hurt.

Slowly, still holding the Pendright, she pushed herself into a sitting position. No nausea, no pounding head. She moved her hand away and remained pain-free. What a wonder or maybe a coincidence? It appeared that the Pendright could protect itself from others, at least.

In the darkness, Kira rose and moved carefully around the chamber, feeling the walls and floors for an exit of some kind. It was a very small room, maybe eight feet long, six feet wide, and eight feet high. The surfaces were all metal and smooth. The entrance was a double door that opened out from the middle. The two men who had come inside only used one door. She'd heard the bolt slide across as they locked her in. There was no easy escape here unless a panel was present in the ceiling that she couldn't reach.

If an hour passed before they returned, it was a very long hour for Kira. In that time, she had developed a ferocious thirst inside her warm, stuffy cell, and her head was on the verge of throbbing again. She was sitting at the far wall facing the door when they opened it and entered. Immediately, the scent of fish chowder flooded her nose, and she began to salivate. She fought to keep her composure and to make her face appear expressionless.

"Oh, so you're awake!" said the gravelly voiced man. Kira noticed he was the shorter of the two and had a thick beard. The other fellow stood behind him, silent.

"Here's some soup for ya," he said and put it on the floor, halfway between Kira and him. "Ya need to drink that down b'fore we leave," he added as he stepped back to the door. His companion remained quiet and continued to stare at Kira. She couldn't make out their features with the light coming in from behind, their faces cast in strong shadow.

Kira moved to a crouch and leaned over to pick up the bowl. It was hot, a metal bowl with no handle or utensils. She moved back to the wall, still crouching and blowing on the soup.

"Can you tell me where we're going?" she asked.

"Ha, you're a funny one!" They both laughed. "No."

Kira sipped her soup. Not bad, she thought, for simple fare. Could have used a bit more salt, perhaps.

"Can you tell me how much longer I'll be inside this cell?" she asked in a matter-of-fact voice and sipped again.

"No, I can't!" The bearded man laughed again. He then growled, "No more questions."

Kira finished her soup slowly. "This isn't a question," she began. "I would like to have some water. Please."

"Huh," he grunted and turned to his companion. "Wally, git 'er some water. A plastic bottle should be okay."

Wally disappeared without a word. Kira pushed her bowl to the middle of the room and leaned back again. The bearded man reached over to pick up the bowl, watching her the entire time. Nothing more was said until Wally returned.

"Here y'are," the bearded man said, setting the bottle in the middle of the floor. Then they stepped out into a corridor and bolted the door shut.

The two men provided a bucket to serve as a chamber pot and appeared every few hours to check on her. They opened the door with great caution each time, giving Kira the impression they expected to be assaulted with the bucket or its contents. She assumed these pirates were probably used to transporting prisoners. Who knew what other contraband they smuggled across the Canada-US border besides kidnap victims like herself? Maybe illegal immigrants, maybe drugs and weapons. Maybe they also fished a little to appear legitimate.

She had a long time to wonder about her fate, about what had happened to her company of merrows. Finally, after vainly trying to imagine how her friends might have escaped to the boats and how Elder Crane's tribe members might have been nearby and helped them beat the Spegars, she cried. She always returned to the worst scenario, with all of them slaughtered, the water murky with their blood. How could they have been so wrong, in spite of their suspicions? She wondered about the true nature and lifestyle of the Spegars. Were they the pirates of the undersea? She began to picture them as slimy green creatures, evil cousins of the finfolk. That did not help her mood one bit as she huddled in the hot, stifling air of her prison cubicle.

By now, she realized, her family might believe she had also died, especially if none of the others with her had survived. Her heart sank when she thought about poor Bess and Cillian, who had already dealt with her numerous disappearances. They were probably sorry they had ever rescued her in the first place. And then there was Cody.

Cody. He would be the one person who still believed in her. He would hold out hope of her survival. He would keep the faith that she would make it. Kira blinked back her tears, again. Yes, she had to keep Cody uppermost in her mind. He wouldn't give up until she was found.

Kira heard faint thudding noises outside, and a few moments later, the door creaked open. When the bearded man set his foot inside, she heard a loud commotion out on the deck. Someone was yelling, and other voices were answering. Was she finally being rescued? Her heart leapt in her chest.

The bearded man stepped toward the bucket in the corner and made a snort of disgust as he picked it up and left, shutting and bolting the door tight. Kira strained to listen to the sounds outside, but her cell walls were well insulated. A few minutes later, she heard the clanging of metal on metal, felt the vibrations of something hitting her walls. Then she felt the cell moving, swaying from side to side. The floor tilted, and she braced herself in a corner so she wouldn't slide. She had to be in a shipping container, the type used to transport goods across the oceans, stacked up on the decks of enormous cargo ships. Where were they taking her now?

Despite her best efforts to stay put, Kira slid across the floor, banging against one wall, and then slid across to the other side. The container came to a sudden shuddering stop. She heard the crane grips come loose and then another thud. She could not tell if her container was next to others, but so far it did not seem that anything had been dropped on top of hers. After a short time had passed, she could not hear or feel any other movement. She did not know whether she was on land or on another ship. She only knew that it was insufferably hot inside and she had run out of water. There was no sense in fretting, she reminded herself. It would only cause her to use up the oxygen in the room and sweat out the precious salt in her body more quickly. She closed her eyes, emptied her head, and willed herself to sleep.

Kira awoke to the steady vibration of engines. They were on the move again. At least it was a little cooler now. However, as the day wore on, the heat radiated into her small cell from the outside. She wondered when anyone would check on her and offer her water at least. She remained curled up on the floor, conserving her air and her strength. Hours later, the door opened and a head poked in. With the brilliant light that flooded in, Kira figured they must be on a deck.

When she tried to speak, she only managed a croak. She cleared her dry throat and tried again. "Water?"

"Kay?" asked the man.

Kira took in a deep breath. "Can I please have water?"

"Ah, el agua," the man nodded. He closed the door and bolted it.

Kira's head felt fuzzy. She knew those words, for she'd learned them at school. What did they mean?

The door opened again a few minutes later, and the man, slender in build, wearing baggy cotton pants and a sleeveless T-shirt, handed Kira a metal cup. *"El agua."*

Of course, *agua* meant "water" in Spanish. Kira took the cup with trembling hands and drank it down in three gulps. She looked up at his dark face. "More? Is there more *agua?"*

He shook his head and took the cup from her hands. *"Más tarde,"* he said, leaving her in darkness again.

Kira lay down and placed both hands on her Pendright. This time it felt cool. She raised the pendant and touched it to her forehead. The coolness spread to her entire head, then down her neck and her back, through her arms and torso, and down her legs to her feet. She breathed in deeply and tasted a cool, salty breeze off the ocean. Kira didn't care whether she was hallucinating or not; she felt normal again.

Eventually, the man returned with more water and a bowl of rice and beans. He also handed her a spoon and then watched as she ate slowly, savouring each mouthful. She'd never eaten rice and beans like these before, nor did she recognize the spices. Without a word, she handed the containers and spoon back to him, and he left. He returned shortly with a bucket.

Over the next hours and days, Kira tried to speak to her assigned caretaker on this vessel, but he only shook his head sadly and said, *"No sé."* He seemed kind, but she had to remind herself that she was a prisoner and he was working for the violent people who paid to have her captured.

When her cell door was opened for the last time, it was dark outside. Several people stood outside on the boat deck, murmuring quietly. A large man stepped inside and growled, *"¡Levantarse!"* as he pulled Kira to her feet. Another man handed him strips of cloth. They tied one around Kira's mouth, another over her eyes, and yet another around her wrists behind her back. Her heart pounded like a drum in her ears. She began to hyperventilate, almost snorting through her nose to get enough air. As they pushed her outside, someone touched Kira's Pendright and then yelped. As terrified as she was, she smiled to herself. Suddenly she felt calm. While the Pendright hung around her neck, she believed she'd be okay.

She could see nothing as she was being led off the boat. The sounds were somewhat familiar and brought to mind her own village wharf. Many of the smells were different, however. Besides the engine fumes, there was a thickly sweet scent in the air, possibly floral, but it reminded her of fruit, citrus or perhaps pineapple. She had only eaten pineapple on a few occasions, and she loved the flavour. Of course, she thought, the Spanish speakers, the hot weather—even the nighttime breeze was warm and sticky. She must be south, far south, perhaps somewhere in the Caribbean. Oh my, how far from home had she travelled?

Eventually, the group accompanying Kira stopped, and she heard a car door opening. She felt like a blind puppet as they pulled her inside, someone on each side of her, pinning her so she could not move. After being cooped up for so long, she was stiff and sore from her walk, which had lasted no longer than ten minutes.

Her captors spoke quietly to each other, but she only understood the odd word. How strange, she thought. She could speak with dolphins, but she couldn't understand most human languages. She had to remind herself that she was not human, and in light of her human captors' cruelty, she took comfort in the fact that she was not one of them.

The car ride did not last long. When they stopped, she heard two car doors opening and then closing. Her backseat companions, however, did not budge. A few minutes later, she heard a tap-tap on the car window and doors opening. She was then dragged from the car and into a building. Her captors escorted her up steps and through echoing hallways; all was silent except for the sounds of their footsteps. Kira tried to keep track of the different sounds made by individual footfalls. She figured there were at least four people walking with her.

They stopped. Kira heard two people approach them. "Aha! *¿Esta es la chica?*"

"*Sí, señor.*"

"*Quitar la venda.*"

Kira felt someone untying her hands, the gag, and, finally, the blindfold.

"*¡Y el resto!*" The man barking the orders stood directly in front of Kira. He was not much taller than she was. He was nearly bald, with a dark mustache and a huge girth that reminded Kira of a pufferfish. His burgundy shirt sparkled under the harsh lights of what appeared to be an office. He smiled at Kira.

"I apologize if my friends have been unkind to you, *chica*. I assure you that we will provide you with a comfortable home here," he said, bowing his head.

"Where am I?" Kira blurted.

The man put his hands together in front of his chin as if he were about to pray. "This detail is not so important. You will be our guest. I promise you will have excellent food to eat and a clean home. The water is refreshed every three days."

"What is this place?" Kira nearly shrieked, trying to keep panic at bay.

The shiny-shirted man simply waved his hand at her and turned away. Kira's two bodyguards steered her out of the office and down a hall, following a woman dressed in a dark-blue uniform. Was this a prison? Were they going to demand a ransom for her?

Kira tried to wiggle free, but her captors tightened their grips on her arms until she felt her hands go numb. She stopped resisting. They continued to walk a labyrinth of halls and stairways and then took an elevator up another level or two. When they emerged from the elevator, they followed the uniformed woman down a corridor to a door that she opened for them. They passed through a narrow room that looked like a kitchen with numerous sinks. The place smelled of fish.

That room opened into another one with a very low ceiling, so they all had to stoop as they entered. Kira could smell and hear lapping water nearby.

"*¡Empujaria en!*" the woman commanded, and Kira's guards pushed her over the lip of a ledge they were standing on. She tumbled several feet down, splashing into a huge tank of water.

Once in the water, Kira felt instant relief to be free of her captors. She swam quickly from one end to the other and back again. However, the feeling of freedom was short-lived. As she drifted to the bottom of the tank in her mermaid form, there, on the other side of the glass, was the puffer man leering at her. He laughed and clapped his hands along with several people standing behind him. Fortunately, Kira could not hear them. She turned her back to them and swam as far away as she could, curling into a ball in a corner. This was even more dreadful than she could ever have imagined. She was a prisoner again, but this time she was trapped in an aquarium for the world to see. She was in a freak show.

Chapter 10 –
Showtime

KIRA DID NOT MOVE from her corner until she noticed that the lights had grown dim. She turned her head slightly—the audience was gone. Far above her, the only lights shone down on the tank, so she decided to swim up for a look. When her head popped out into air, she lay on her back to float on the surface and get her bearings. The walls on three sides of the tank were made of concrete and covered with a slick blue, like boat paint. The ledge she had been pushed from was at least eight feet higher than the water surface. Above her on all sides, there were smooth concrete walls, and the ceiling had three pot lights. The glass wall opposite the ledge started just below the water surface on the fourth side. She figured it went down about twenty feet to the floor of the aquarium.

For several minutes, Kira closed her eyes and listened closely as she floated on the water. She heard no sounds that would suggest someone might be on the deck above her or in the adjoining narrow room with sinks. "Hello!" she yelled. The echo bounced once before it was swallowed. "Anyone there?"

Kira waited in silence a few minutes longer before diving down to the bottom of the tank. She hovered near the floor and then beat her tail hard and drove herself up through the water, piercing the surface with her arms fully extended and reaching for the ledge. Her hands smacked the wall, at least a foot short. She slipped back into the water.

She had misjudged the height above the water. It had to be at least a ten-foot drop, not eight. Fully stretched out, Kira knew she measured about eight feet long from the tips of her extended fingers to the edge of her tail fin. She needed to clear the water by at least two feet to reach the ledge. She was disappointed at her failure, but it was only her first attempt. Kira was determined to build up her strength so she could escape her aquarium prison. In the last couple of years, she had spent very little time in the water. She was out of shape. She would exercise and eat well. The puffer man mentioned she'd be well fed. She would get out of here, she promised herself.

For now, Kira decided to explore the entire tank for another potential exit. She wondered how they refreshed the water every three days, for instance. There were a few fish swimming in the tank. Were they meant to be her food? Along the floor, there were several seaweeds anchored in sand. A fake coral was situated near the middle of the floor, along with two corals painted on the back wall. The paintings were rather well done, Kira thought. She didn't recognize the seaweeds or the fish species in the tank, but she was in the tropics, so that was not surprising. Nor was the water temperature, which was several degrees warmer than her home waters in the northern Atlantic.

She shook her head and continued to explore her new home. Temporary home, she reminded herself. The tank was about thirty feet long and six feet wide. She found a circular disc that protruded from one end about three feet off the ground. She felt a rush of water coming out from behind the disc. At the opposite end, water flowed toward another similar disc that was about five feet off the ground. This had to be the drain where water slipped around the disk and into a grate in the wall itself. So this was the water-refreshing system the shiny puffer man had mentioned.

In spite of her exhaustion, Kira's brain was in overdrive. If she could not jump out of the water, perhaps she could raise the level of the water in the aquarium by blocking the drain for a while. However, she'd first have to learn the work patterns of her keepers: when they arrived, their schedules during the day, and when they finished work. It was night now, and there did not seem to be anyone around. It was a large building, though, and they probably had security guards outside and possibly inside as well. Or perhaps they had purposely led her around a few extra laps to make her think the facility was larger than it really was so that she'd be less inclined to attempt an escape.

Then again, she was probably overthinking things. Kira closed her eyes as she settled on the bottom near a back corner. She'd have a better idea of what might be possible once she learned the routines. Patience, that's what she needed now. She had to stay positive, she thought. She had to banish all those images of captive dolphins and seals, separated from their pods and herds, their parents, siblings, and babies, ultimately languishing and dying in aquariums around the world. She was determined that this would not happen to her. No way! There was no question in her mind that she'd rather die than live in captivity. But right now, she needed to stay strong, to be calm, and to sleep.

***

A SHRILL WHISTLE startled Kira awake. When she opened her eyes, the brightness made her squint. Was it morning already? How long had she slept? She peeked out beyond the glass and could see several people staring in, pointing at her. A child had his face up against the glass, his eyes wide with wonder. Kira turned away again and curled up tightly. They would have to make do with staring at her back. She was not going to entertain anyone. After a few minutes, she heard the shrill whistle again. It was nothing like dolphin sounds; it had to be man-made. Kira glanced up to the top of the tank. A face was looking down over the ledge. She watched as a small box was lowered into the water. When the whistle sounded again, Kira fought the urge to swim up and yell at this person. If they wanted her to swim and show off to the audience, this method would not work. She would show them that she was not a trained zoo animal.

She tucked her head down and put her hands over her ears. She could still hear the whistle every few minutes. This was torture. Kira remembered reading about all the damage humans were doing to sea mammals with their underwater seismic testing. She could understand how that would drive them crazy, considering how their hearing worked. At least she had hands to dampen the sound somewhat.

After what seemed like hours, the whistles stopped. Kira was stiff and cramped where she huddled. She yearned to stretch her long mermaid body. She took another peek behind her. There did not seem to be anyone in the room, but she could not see into the darkened corners. As her eyes adjusted, she felt more certain that she was alone. She glanced up and saw no one looking down at her, either. She carefully unfolded herself and then swam slowly to the surface. She listened and thought she heard rustling above her.

"Hello? Anyone there?" she called.

The rustling stopped. She heard footsteps, followed by a buzz, and then a woman speaking, probably in Spanish. Kira could not make out her words.

"Hello!" she called again. "Hola," she added in Spanish. She wished she knew more than the few words she'd learned at school.

A door opened and closed, and footsteps grew louder. A woman's head peered over the ledge above her. Kira recognized her as the woman in the blue suit from yesterday.

"So, you are awake now, yes?"

"Yes," Kira said. "Why are you blowing that whistle, and why am I in here?" she demanded, irritated by the woman's casual attitude, as if Kira were a child who had slept in.

The woman smiled. "You only need to do some swimming, and we won't sound the whistle. This is not so hard to do."

"I will not perform for anyone while I am a prisoner. I would like to leave. Immediately!"

"This is not possible. If you refuse to move, that is your choice. But you will receive no food. You are free to choose."

Kira gasped. "You want me to die in here?"

"Of course not, *chica loca*," the woman laughed.

"But that's what will happen when I choose to starve. What kind of monsters are you?" Kira dove back under, furious and frightened. Would they really let her starve?

She settled behind the fake coral and leaned her back against the wall. Still no one had reappeared on the other side of the glass. She was ready to burst into tears of frustration, but she was too angry to cry. She looked around at the few fish flitting by. There was enough food to last a couple of days, she supposed. How long could she hold out after that? She had two days to figure out how to escape, though she suspected that the doors would be locked even if she managed to get out of the tank. She was probably doomed.

Later that night, once the lights had been dimmed, Kira darted around the tank, catching fish and eating her fill. She hadn't realized how hungry she'd been. Then she gathered strips of seaweed and slipped them behind the disc covering the outflow of the tank. It did not take long for all the openings to be plugged. Because she didn't know how fast the water was flowing in, she had no idea how long it would take for the water level to rise by at least one foot. If the workers noticed the water rising when they lowered the noisemaker, they would probably investigate it and turn off the tap.

Kira decided that at least for the next day, she would pretend to cooperate and swim around for them. In fact, she would be awake and on the move before anyone arrived so they wouldn't have to sound the morning whistle. She slept very little that night, swimming up to the surface several times to see if the water level had changed. She thought it did, but only by two or three inches. That was perfect. She didn't want to alert anyone too soon.

Just before the lights went on the next morning, Kira noticed that the level had increased by at least six inches; her plan was working. She was about to resume her slow circling of the pool when she heard the door to the tank room opening and footsteps approaching the ledge. A shower of fish suddenly dropped out of an overturned bucket. Whoever dumped them did not bother to look over the ledge.

"Excellent!" she thought as she dove after the scattering fish. She was not hungry, just excited, until she saw the shiny-shirted puffer man on the other side of the glass. She stopped short and, for an instant, thought about sticking her tongue out at him. It would have made her feel better, but she didn't want to acknowledge him in any way or to attract attention to herself.

She continued to swim, occasionally glancing sideways to see if anyone was watching. A steady stream of people wandered by, always stopping to stare. Some of the adults pointed at her and laughed. They shook their heads when they talked to their children, waving their hands dismissively. Of course, they were explaining there was no such thing as a real mermaid and that what they saw in the tank was just a fancy trick.

This was just as well, thought Kira. If more people knew the truth, they'd be searching for merrows and hunting them for various purposes including entertainment. Perhaps that era and the end of merrows everywhere were not far off. At this dark thought, Kira swam up to the surface and floated for a while. Then she dove down, grabbed a fish, and began to eat it, head first. When she looked out through the glass, she was face to face with a woman who was surrounded by children. The woman stood horrified with her mouth agape. Kira, still chewing, raised a hand and waved at them, her other hand still holding the bottom half of the bleeding fish. The woman turned and began to shoo her children away from the exhibit. Kira watched them hurry off, the children with their mouths forming pink O's, straining to look behind them. Kira smiled. She was feeling wicked and satisfied. Those folks got their money's worth anyway. She wondered how the mother would explain that "trick" to her children.

By the time the crowds had disappeared and the lights were dimmed, Kira was exhausted. She had not slept much the night before, and she was anxious about the rising water, hoping no one would bother to check on her. When enough time had passed, she swam to the surface and listened. Except for the pot lights above her, there were no other lights on and no sounds of people nearby. It's time, she thought.

She swam to the bottom and looked out again. The viewing room was dark and empty. She beat her tail hard and shoved off, shooting up along the back wall, her arms extended. As she broke through the surface, she beat her tail even harder and flew up through the air. She was going to make it! Her fingers hooked over the ledge as her upward momentum slowed to a stop. However, only the tips made contact, and even though her tail had morphed to legs, she could not grip the slippery wall to boost herself up farther. She slid back down into the water.

"No!" she shouted and then swam back down. She needed more speed, which meant a longer takeoff. Kira positioned herself in a corner by the glass. This time she pushed away from the side wall as she launched herself diagonally across the tank and beat her tail as hard as possible, exploding into the air and up the wall, landing on the ledge with her upper body, and sliding the rest of the way onto the solid surface. She lay there quietly, stilling her heart and her breathing. She felt warmth radiating from her Pendright and clutched it with both hands. There was no light coming from beneath the door to the adjoining room. She moved into a crouch and stood up slowly. She was dripping on the tiles, but she was now certain no one was in the adjoining room. Still, she tiptoed quietly and opened the door to the sink room.

Kira let her eyes adjust to the dark. Without her glasses, she was at a disadvantage, but there was nothing to be done about it. She crept to the door leading out into the hall, turned the handle, and pulled. It was locked. She pulled harder, twisting the handle back and forth, but it would not give. There were no windows in that room, no other exit. She returned to the tank room and explored it carefully. There was not much to look at, just the walls and a low ceiling with lights. No trap doors, nothing. She was stuck inside.

Kira sat on the floor and considered her options. If she remained where she was, she could surprise anyone who came in. In fact, if she hid behind the tank room door and someone walked in with a bucket of fish, for instance, she could push them into the water and get herself out the door and into the hall. Then she'd need to find a way out of the building during the day. However, an escape in broad daylight would be risky, for anyone spotting a sopping-wet girl would likely be suspicious—that is, if they didn't recognize her first. Plus, it wouldn't take long for them to notice down below that she was no longer in the aquarium. There was no place to hide in the tank.

She decided to take her chances with a morning escape, which was her only option other than jumping back into the tank. By morning, she'd be somewhat drier anyway and maybe not as noticeable. She made herself as comfortable as she could on the hard, cold floor.

Kira awoke when she heard the click of the hall door being unlocked. She stood up quietly and then walked behind the closed door. A few seconds later, a woman opened the door to the tank room and stepped inside with a bucket. As she leaned over slightly to dump the fish, Kira thought of just running around the door and into the hallway. However, if the woman saw her, she'd call for help, a risk that Kira could not afford. Back to the first plan, Kira slipped out from behind the door and pushed the woman just as she was turning around with her empty bucket.

"¡No sé nadar!" screamed the woman as she fell backward into the pool.

Kira heard the splash and hesitated. She'd heard that phrase before, but what did it mean? She had to look over the ledge before she left. With dismay, Kira immediately recognized a frightening flaw in her plan, something she should have considered before pushing anyone into deep water. The woman was thrashing and sinking. She couldn't swim!

Kira dove in and brought her back to the surface. The woman coughed, hiccupped, and began to cry. Feeling terrible, Kira wanted more than anything to have the woman back on the ledge before anyone discovered them.

"I'm going to get you back up there. Put your hands here, on the wall. I'm going to push you out." Kira pointed up, not sure if the woman understood her. She lowered herself underwater while propping her up, placed the woman's feet on her two shoulders, and then lifted her up out of the water along the wall. The woman hugged the wall and walked her hands up as Kira pushed from below. With a final shove, the woman was hoisted up onto the ledge.

Kira drifted back down, thoroughly dispirited. She had almost killed someone, a worker who probably knew little about Kira, who probably didn't even know she had been abducted against her will. And now any small hope of escape had evaporated.

She swam slowly around the tank to calm her racing heart. She was picturing the worker telling her bosses that the mermaid was dangerous. Would they punish Kira by putting her in a more secure and even smaller aquarium? And what if they didn't believe the employee? After all, Kira was still in the tank and had never left it as far as they knew. Perhaps the woman wouldn't say anything. However, in case she did, Kira decided to remove all evidence of her tampering with the drain.

She looked out the glass into the viewing area. There were still no spectators, so she swam to the drain. Keeping her eyes focused on the room, she slid a hand behind the disc cover and rubbed at the seaweed clogging the openings. She managed to dislodge little bits of green slime from the drain with her fingers. The smaller pieces were sucked into the drain holes. She could feel the strong flow of water resume. Assuming the rate into the drain matched the rate of incoming water on the other side, she figured that the level at the top should remain the same—not that she was planning another attempt to jump out anytime soon.

A few moments later, the aquarium oglers began to arrive. Kira observed them from the corners of her eyes, but otherwise she ignored them as she swam around the tank. She did not catch and eat any fish to entertain the audience that day. She decided she'd eat only at night as long as she planned to stay alive. She didn't want to think too far ahead into the future. The only thing Kira did know for certain was that she would never grow old in that aqueous prison.

Chapter 11 –
A Favour Repaid

AS FAR AS KIRA COULD TELL, either the woman who brought her fish every day never told her employers about being pushed into the tank, or they didn't care. If the same person came each day, she would probably be much more cautious when entering the tank room. A few days after the incident, Kira decided to find out.

She was waiting at the surface when the morning lights came on. Kira heard the door to the tank room opening, and she called out, "Hello! ¡Hola!"

The person had stopped. Kira backed up to the wall opposite the ledge and could just make her out in the shadows, standing still, holding a bucket. Kira raised her hand and waved it. "It's okay. *Lo siento*. I don't mean to scare you." She'd been working to remember the few Spanish words and phrases she knew.

The woman took a step closer and peered down. Kira recognized the face of the person she had nearly drowned. The worker leaned over slightly, keeping her eyes on Kira while she emptied the bucket. Some of Kira's favourite fish flew out and twisted in the air before they splashed down and disappeared below. The woman straightened up and said, "Hola," without smiling. At least she spoke, Kira thought.

"Do you speak any English?"

The woman shook her head and then said, "Only little."

"I just want to say I'm sorry about what happened. I really am." In case anyone else was listening, Kira didn't mention any details of their first encounter.

"Is okay," the woman said.

Kira expelled a huge breath of relief. "My name is, uh, Coralene," she said, suddenly deciding to borrow a name. "What is your name?"

"It's Rosa."

"A beautiful name." Kira smiled up at her. "Do you have children, Rosa?"

"*Sí. Dos,* two. Boy and girl."

Kira took a deep breath, encouraged by Rosa's willingness to talk. "How old are they?"

Rosa looked confused for a moment.

"Um, how many years, your boy and girl?" she rephrased.

Rosa put down the bucket and raised her hands. "Boy," she said and showed six fingers. "Girl." Ten fingers spread wide.

"Okay, so your boy is six and your girl is ten."

She nodded. *"Sí."*

"I am nearly eighteen years old," Kira said, pointing to herself and showing all ten fingers and then eight. Rosa's face looked more relaxed as she nodded. Kira thought carefully about what she would say next. She spoke slowly.

"My mother and my father are afraid. They do not know I am here. I want to go home." Kira sniffed to hold in her tears.

Rosa frowned and then her hands went up into the air. She muttered in Spanish, shaking her head. *"¡Lo siento!* I think you come day. Go home night. I think *sirena* is no true! I think this is show, not real. *No sé.* Sorry!"

"It's okay, Rosa. I just want to go home. I miss my family. They probably think I'm dead." Kira stopped, not wanting to beg for help. The poor woman had no power or authority, and she looked miserable, wringing her hands.

"I go," she said and picked up her bucket.

"Adios, Rosa. Gracias for talking to me."

Rosa left, still muttering.

Now they were both unhappy, Kira thought. She sank back underwater, resumed her cruising show speed and made a vertical loop around the tank. Rosa seemed to have a conscience and a good heart. Realizing that Kira was a prisoner had upset her, and obviously learning that *sirenas*, "mermaids," were real must have been a shock. Perhaps Rosa was also a prisoner of sorts and needed this job to support her family. She may have said nothing to her employers about the escape attempt for fear of being fired.

When Rosa walked into the tank room the next day, Kira was at the surface again, waiting for her. "*Buenas dias*, Rosa," Kira said, practising one of her remembered phrases.

Rosa gave a small start when she first saw Kira and then smiled a little. "*Buenas dias,* Coralena," she responded and then upturned the bucket of fish into the tank.

"Where do these fish come from, Rosa?"

"The sea."

"Which sea? I don't know where we are."

"Oh?" Rosa seemed surprised.

"I come from the northern Atlantic. From Canada."

"*¿Sí*? So far? This is Panama City," Rosa said.

"Panama! Wow, that is far from home. No wonder it took so long." Kira's memory flashed back to the metal container she'd lived in for uncountable days. The aquarium was certainly better than that.

"Can you tell me about this place? Are there other displays here? Do they have animals in tanks like this one?"

"*Sí*, there are many. Big fish, little fish. *Anguilas*, you know, like snakes in sea?"

"Ah, eels? What else?"

"*Pulpo*, you know, with many arms." Rosa waved her arms around and then held up eight fingers.

"Octopus? Oh no, not octopuses. They are such intelligent creatures." Kira was picturing her friend, the giant Sherman. "What is the name of this place, this aquarium?"

"Acuario Científica de Panamá. For people to come, to learn. And there are *cocodrilos, tortugas*. Many sea animals," Rosa said, opening her arms wide.

"And one *sirena*," Kira added. "Or are there others like me?"

"No, *chica*, one," she said sadly.

The outside door opened, and a male voice called out, "Rosa? *¿Estás ahí?*"

Rosa jumped and replied, *"Sí. ¡Yo vengo de inmediato!"* She waved at Kira and left.

Kira swam back down and resumed her loopy cruising, back and forth and around. So this was her life now, that of a caged animal, pacing in the water like all the other thousands of zoo animals around the world. She swore to herself that if she managed to escape, she would campaign for the closing of all such facilities everywhere. She would begin with the sea mammals as well as octopuses and continue until all other sensitive, thinking animals were free. She'd draw the line at creatures like finfolk and Spegars. She was more certain than ever that the latter were not true merrows at all.

After several days of brief morning talks with Rosa, Kira was surprised to learn that Rosa worked seven days a week, with shifts starting at six in the morning and ending at noon. Most days she also worked as a waitress in a nearby restaurant. Her husband was a truck driver for a fresh seafood company that made deliveries throughout Central America.

As much as she enjoyed chatting with Rosa and learning Spanish while Rosa improved her English, Kira was growing more anxious about how much longer she could tolerate her living conditions. Every night, she dreamt about being with her parents, or visiting Jimmy and his goats, or sailing on a research vessel with Cody as he scurried about in a white laboratory coat. Once she dreamt about Janus. They were swimming underwater, exploring the sea bottom for exotic Caribbean plants until some dark monster interrupted them. She awoke, her heart pounding.

Most of all, Kira missed being on land and having legs again. Every morning, she awoke more depressed and had to force herself to swim in figure eights and eat her fish. She was losing her appetite. She began to eat less, grew more tired, and spent more time resting than swimming.

One day Rosa commented, "You do not eat all the fish. You are *flaco, delgado.*"

Kira shrugged. "I'm not hungry. I have so little to do. Just bring fewer fish."

"Oh no, they say you must eat all the fish. They will be angry."

"You know what, Rosa? I don't care. They told me I had a choice— to eat or not to eat. I don't want to eat. I think I want to...to sleep and not wake up until I'm home. Or not ever wake up again." Kira surprised herself with those words, but she knew they were true. This was not living. This was simply existing, and that was not enough for her. All her loved ones thought she was dead anyway.

Kira could hear Rosa shouting as she drifted down to the bottom and lay on the floor, her back to the glass. This was the end for her, and she really didn't care.

The next morning, Kira swam up just to see Rosa. Her friend was frowning with worry when she greeted Kira.

"They told me not to bring fish today, because you do not swim. You must swim. You must eat," she scolded like the concerned mother she was.

"Oh, Rosa, I'm sorry. I don't want to make your life any harder, but I have no appetite. The thought of putting anything into my mouth makes me nauseous."

"You are sick! Maybe we call a doctor?"

"Like who? A veterinarian? Ha! They can't let me out of here. I'm a prisoner! This is a jail!"

"Shh!" Rosa said. "No dying!" She clutched the cross hanging from her neck and looked behind her quickly. "Maybe we can help you," she whispered, "to go away." She stared down at Kira, her eyes wide and frightened.

"We? Who can help me, Rosa?" Kira could not be hearing right. Her brain must be playing tricks on her.

Rosa closed the door to the tank room and then leaned way over the ledge. "My husband, he knows someone. Can take you to United States."

Kira's mouth fell open. Now she knew she was hearing things.

"When I tell him that you are true *sirena*, he says there is *científico* who ask for *sirena*, for mermaid, if we find. And—no, I think no," Rosa said, beginning to cry.

"What is it, Rosa? What are you saying?"

Rosa sobbed, "I no want you to die." She took out a rag from her pocket and blew her nose. "I not know where you go in United States. They pay money. No good. Is *peligroso*. Danger!"

"But Rosa, if I can get out of here, maybe I can escape and go home. At least I'd have a chance."

Rosa shook her head.

"Rosa, I will die in here. I'll take any other chance I can get. Please!"

"No! No die!" Rosa turned and fled from the room.

Kira was not sure what Rosa meant. But if she would at least help her escape the aquarium, then she'd need to keep up her strength to break free from the next set of hands on her. A scientist looking for mermaids might be more promising than being part of a circus, as long as she didn't become a specimen for dissection. She shuddered at the thought. She had two choices: face the unknown or fade away under her current circumstances. She was desperate. If she were offered an exit, she would take her chances.

Kira swam a few loops and forced herself to eat a couple of smaller fish in plain view of her audience. Several children clapped their hands and laughed. Only one little girl made a face, but she was all eyes and didn't turn away. The adults were predictably grossed out. After fasting for a few days, she felt pain in her stomach when she ate the first few small fish. However, the cramping did not last long, and soon she began to perk up. She focused on the thought of seeing daylight again, or at least being able to breathe the air outside, even for a short while. The atmosphere above the tank was stale, with a chemical odour she didn't recognize. That night she slept fitfully, wondering if she would see Rosa the next morning and if Rosa had made up the story to get Kira to eat. No, she didn't think Rosa was capable of being that cruel, and, anyway, a deception like that couldn't last long.

Rosa was there to greet Kira when she popped up after the lights went on. Still no bucket of fish, she noticed.

"They said you have many fish still. They are happy you eat."

"I'm only eating if I can get out of here, right?"

Rosa gave a heavy sigh. "Yes. Tomorrow I come, maybe with fish. Next day, someone else. I go to my mother's village. She is *enferma*, uh, sick. You understand?"

"*Sí*, Rosa, I understand."

Rosa frowned and her mouth trembled. She clutched her cross and left.

Kira ate several fish that day and swam more loops than usual. When she saw Rosa the next morning, she was carrying the fish bucket.

"Four small fish today. There are still many in water," she said as she dumped them in.

"Yes, I'm feeling stronger today. I should be able to make the jump tomorrow. Anything I need to know?"

"I leave new clothes for you. Uniform like me. Put on before you go, and take old clothes away. When he come, you go in laundry basket. Big basket, on wheels."

"A laundry cart," Kira said with a grin, as if they were having one of their language lessons.

"Sí, un carro de lavandería," she said, her smile tentative. "He take outside to *camion.*"

"A truck! In daylight. I hope no one notices."

"He come early, no lights inside, is dark outside. Will be okay." But Rosa's expression was anxious, not at all confident.

"Can you wait for a moment, Rosa? I want to try something. Don't be afraid, okay? Nothing bad will happen." Kira waited for Rosa to nod, though she still looked worried.

Kira dove down to a far corner and immediately turned around and hurled herself up through the water to the far side. As she launched into the air, she saw Rosa step back with her hand over her cross. When Kira landed on the floor, Rosa stood in the corner, shaking, her eyes wide.

Kira quickly jumped to her feet and opened her arms. "I just wanted to thank you, Rosa, if you'll let me. I don't expect I'll ever see you again."

Rosa nodded, still speechless. Kira approached her slowly and then wrapped her dripping wet arms around the shivering woman.

"Rosa, you probably won't understand everything I say, but whatever happens, I know you are a good person. I'll always be grateful to you. I'm sure everything will work out, and I'll get home again. Please don't worry. And don't feel guilty about the money they pay. Use it for yourself and your children."

Rosa squeezed Kira in a tight embrace. Then she gently pushed the wet girl away. "You go. They miss you, will be trouble." She sniffled and pointed down to the water.

"Adios, Rosa. *¡Y muchas* gracias!" Kira dove in without looking back.

Chapter 12 –
Sea to Sea

ONCE THE LIGHTS WENT OUT, Kira found she could not sleep. She decided to jump up out of the tank so her hair might dry off before her "ride" showed up. After landing on the ledge, she removed her old, worn clothing and slipped into the one-piece blue uniform. She curled up in a corner and closed her eyes.

All was still in darkness when she heard a key turning in the outside door. Kira remained still and watched the tank room door open slowly. A tall man in the standard blue uniform stepped inside. He approached the ledge with caution, leaned over, and peered into the tank. Kira had a sudden vision of herself locked in a dank dungeon. She imagined pushing him into the water and running out by herself. As if sensing her thoughts, the man turned his head and looked straight at her.

"¿Quién es usted?" he growled.

"I'm your passenger. *Pasajero*," she repeated, pointing at herself as she watched his face.

He nodded, visibly relieved, and waved her forward. He picked up her old clothing and stuffed it into a waste bag he had brought along. Once he checked the corridor, Kira followed him outside. He pulled a pile of towels and uniforms out of the laundry cart and then pointed at it. Kira scrambled inside and crouched down while he threw the laundry back on top of her. She found herself holding her breath as the cart began to move. When she resumed breathing, the faint fishy odour of the towels drifted up her nose. She began to sweat under all the layers. The trip was taking a long time, she thought, with endless turns around corners. They stopped abruptly.

Kira heard beeps, followed by mechanical noises. She then felt a jolt before they stopped again. Suddenly the cart was falling. They were on an elevator, of course. She wanted to laugh but stifled the urge. Nerves. She had to remain calm and silent. She felt for the Pendright and immediately sensed her heartbeat slowing down.

More rolling, swaying around corners, doors opening and closing. Kira heard muffled voices through the layers. After another big bump, she felt herself tilting sideways. This time, she really was falling. She then landed with a soft thump on a bed of sour-smelling laundry. She tore at the towels on top of her and poked out of a hill of damp cloth. It was dark grey outside, but she could see lamps shining behind the open back of the truck. A second later, the back doors of the truck creaked and slammed shut, blocking out all light. She heard two doors close and an engine roar. The smell of gasoline wafted through the air around her. She fell toward the back as the truck lurched forward. Kira dug herself into the laundry again, not certain if she was supposed to remain hidden. A few more instructions would have been helpful.

Between the jerky stops and starts and the pungent fumes, Kira was glad her flipping stomach was empty. She listened to the sounds of city traffic outside: the bleating horns, occasional whistles, people shouting. It was morning in Panama City. She was out in the real world again, yet here she was stuck inside a moving holding cell. She prayed it would be temporary.

They stopped again after about half an hour of driving. Kira listened intently as doors opened and shut and people talked. The traffic sounds were muted now. Was this a transfer point? Finally, one of the back doors opened, and two men stood against the grey light of dawn, looking in. These two also wore uniforms, but they appeared to be khaki coloured. There was no sign of the man who had rolled her to the truck.

One of the men waved her forward. "Come," he said. "You like some breakfast?" he asked and smiled as Kira crawled over the laundry toward them. She noticed he had a mustache and the other man simply had stubble and wore a bored expression.

"Maybe later," she said, taking the hands they offered to help her out.

The mustached man said, "Sure, we have time. Come!" The tone was friendly, but the way they each gripped her arms was all business. They steered her toward one of the many drab buildings along the side of a river. Kira saw the lights of several large boats moored nearby. It was wonderful to be waterside once again and possible escape. She paid close attention to where they were heading and what was around them. She was relieved that at least this Hispanic man spoke excellent English.

"Um, where are we?" she asked.

"Aha, welcome to the Panama Canal!" said the mustached man, opening a door and guiding her inside. They walked Kira past an empty counter and down a hallway, finally opening the door to a room with a long table and several chairs.

"You can wait here in our customs office. We have some paperwork to finish." Kira noted that other than the table, chairs, and a wastebasket, the concrete room was windowless and completely empty.

Kira sat in a chair. "How long will I be here?"

"Hmm, a few hours. I need to check the ship schedule. Would you like some coffee or tea?"

"Uh, tea would be fine, thank you." Kira couldn't remember when she last drank tea. She had never taken to coffee.

"Sugar, miss? Sorry, there is no milk." He beamed a smile at Kira that almost seemed genuine. She wondered how much money he made at this security job.

"Tea without milk is fine, thanks." Why was she being so polite when she was being held captive?

The two men left, the click of the door suggesting that Kira was locked in. She listened for their footsteps to fade before she stood up and tested the door handle. Locked, of course, but at least she was no longer on display in an aquarium. Kira grimaced and sighed. She would have to enjoy the moment, enjoy having her legs again as long as it lasted.

The tea, contained in a waxy paper cup, did not appear for some time—at least half an hour, she figured. And it was tepid. Her mouth was as parched as paper, and she drank it down in three gulps. Kira wondered what had happened to the breakfast she'd been offered. Another hour must have passed by before the door opened again, and the mustached man reappeared with a Styrofoam plate of food.

"This is what I can find. Some papaya, melon, cheese, and a bread roll. Very healthy. Do you eat fruit?" he asked and cocked his head as if he were looking at an alien. How much did he know about her? She was definitely an alien in this place; that was certain.

"Yes, this looks great. Do you think I could have more tea or just plain water?" She smiled at him.

"Of course!" he said as he was leaving. She noticed he did not ever completely turn his back on her as he exited the room and he had not provided her with any cutlery. He returned within minutes, holding a large Styrofoam cup of water. As she prepared to leave again, she stopped him.

"Is there a restroom I can use?"

He gave her a confused look.

"Um, you know, a *baño*? Bathroom?"

"Ah, sí. Yes. Wait a moment," he said and left.

He returned a few minutes later and said, "Come with me." Kira stood up and walked down a corridor with him. He stopped at a door with the symbol of a woman and then nodded. Kira walked inside. It was a small bathroom with one metal sink and one toilet stall. There were no windows and no other exits other than the door she'd entered. She sighed, used the toilet, washed her hands and her face, and then pulled on the door handle to leave. The door did not budge.

She tapped on the door. "Hello out there! I'm ready to go!" She waited until the door swung open, and the mustached man nodded at her. All this time she'd been looking for any opportunity to run, though she didn't know if she could get out of the building or what she'd find once she was outside. There didn't seem to be many people around. This building was rather quiet for a customs or cargo business, probably because it was neither.

This time, the man's smile seemed strained. Kira wondered what he normally did and how often he guarded and accompanied undocumented immigrants or criminals. Or kidnap victims like herself. Obviously, this smiley, mustached man was involved in human trafficking. Just thinking those words made her shudder. She'd never dreamt that anything like this could ever happen to her, a fisher's daughter from a tiny village in Atlantic Canada.

Kira walked silently back with the guard to the "customs" office. When he left, she put her arms on the table, laid down her head, and began to cry. After a few deep sobs, Kira raised her head again and wiped her sleeves across her wet cheeks. Crying would not help her escape. She had to remain strong. She picked up a piece of melon and began to eat, her first meal out of water in weeks. The fruit was sweet and juicy and helped get the dry bread roll and cheese down her throat. She drank all the water and put down her cup.

Kira stared at her hands spread out on the table in front of her. How many fingers? Had she grown more fingers? She chuckled.

Suddenly she couldn't focus on anything, and her head felt like it was full of rocks. Kira laid it back down on the table and closed her eyes.

Kira was lost in a deep, dark ocean trench. She couldn't remember how she got there, only that she had been swimming away from a dangerous green creature. It was round and spiny, seemingly taking twisted delight in brandishing its long, sharp claws and clacking its knife-like teeth together. In this lightless abyss, she could not see where she was going or if the monster was closing in on her. She flailed her arms as she spun around and around, staring desperately into the black water but seeing nothing. Was she blind?

Kira cracked her eyes open, and grey light began to filter in. Her head spinning, she felt waves of nausea sweep over her. She closed her eyes quickly. She could sense vibrations where she lay, could feel the cloth beneath her. Was she on a bed, her own bed? She opened her eyes, slowly this time, until the spinning stopped and she could focus again. She was in a cramped room, dark except for weak light sifting in through a small oval window above her. The humming and vibrations were familiar. She closed her eyes again and listened. She was on a ship.

Kira rose carefully from her cot and looked out the smudged, head-sized window. She tried to rub off the dirt with her sleeve; however, when she focused more closely, she realized that wire mesh had been embedded in the glass. Outside, the sky was cloudy. She could just make out a fuzzy dark streak on the horizon—a shoreline, perhaps. As she watched, the horizon shifted at the pace of a creeping starfish. Kira tried to remember where she'd been before she ended up in the cabin. Her brain was as dull as the day outside and moved about as fast as the plodding ship. She lay down and, within moments, was asleep again.

Kira dreamt of sitting down to a hot meal of chowder and fresh baked bread. She was reaching for the butter dish when she awoke and bolted upright. The room was black; night had fallen. She smelled food, real food. As her eyes adjusted to the dark, she noticed something on a shelf by the door that had not been there earlier. Kira stood up and approached it. She found herself salivating as she stood over a plate of mixed beans and rice. There was something soft and pliable next to it, a flatbread or tortilla. Next to the plate stood a large bottle of liquid. She opened the cap and sniffed—no odour, probably water. What was safe to eat or drink? She was pretty sure now that the food or drink at the "customs" office must have been spiked with some kind of sedative.

Kira sat on the edge of her cot and used the folded tortilla to scoop beans and rice into her mouth. She didn't know what seasonings were used to spice the mixture, but it was delicious. She ate it all, every bean and every grain of rice.

When she finished, she looked around for a waste bucket and was surprised to see a small toilet in the corner of her tiny room. Even more shocking, she could flush it. She had moved up in the world of captive transport, from shipping container to laundry truck to a mini ensuite cabin.

She took the bottle to her cot and lay down. There was nothing to do but empty her mind and wait for morning or for her captors' next move. There was no point in thinking about what might happen to her. There were worse scenarios than being trapped in an aquarium, but she didn't want to go there. She was miserable enough already. Kira took a deep breath and closed her eyes.

A knock on the door woke her up. Kira's eyes popped open, but she lay quietly in the cot. Another knock.

"¡Hola! *¡Buenas dias!*" The door opened a crack at first and then widened as a stocky woman in a cream-coloured shirt and pants slipped in with a loaded tray. After closing the door behind her, she glanced at Kira, who had squeezed her eyes nearly shut. The woman then set a food-laden plate down on the shelf next to the empty one. She remained by the door, staring down at Kira.

"Awake?" she asked.

Kira opened her eyes and looked up at the woman, standing less than three feet away. She supposed that her captors wanted to make sure she was still alive, though the woman would have guessed it from the empty plate.

"Yes, I'm awake."

"I brought you breakfast," she said. "You liked the *gallo pinto?*" She picked up the empty plate and grinned at Kira.

Kira sat up. The woman acted like she wanted to befriend her. Kira rubbed her eyes, trying to decide what to do. She had two options available to her: she could be either friendly in return or surly and uncooperative. She didn't know where she was going or what her new "buyers" wanted from her. She might learn more if she pretended to be friendly, might earn privileges, might find a way to escape.

Kira forced a smile. "Yes, the rice and beans were delicious. What were the spices?"

"Ahh, that is a special salsa. It is called Lizano, from Costa Rica. In Panama, we add more tamarind, so it is just a little different."

Kira nodded her head. She really didn't care about the salsa, but she kept her lips pressed together and smiling.

"I brought you eggs with beans, no rice. And toast." The woman pointed to each item as if she were trying to make a sale. "Do you eat eggs?"

"Yes, I eat eggs and toast," Kira said. She swallowed the saliva filling her mouth. "My name is Coralene. What's your name?"

The woman's smile wavered for a second, and then she said, "My name is Selena."

Kira stared at the woman, wondering if she was making fun of her. Had she just called herself "Sirena," the Spanish word for mermaid?

"You know Selena, the famous Mexican-American singer? The girl who died so young? The same name."

Kira sighed. "Yes, of course. Such a sad story."

Selena nodded and then pointed to the tray. "You must eat now, or it will get cold. Will you take tea or coffee?"

"Maybe I'll have tea later. Water is fine for now. A large bottle, please. It's very warm in this room." Kira handed her the empty plastic bottle.

Selena took it and then left. Kira noticed that she did not turn her back on Kira for a moment. Kira tested the door handle—locked, as she had expected.

She picked up the plate of food and sat at the edge of her cot. A blue plastic spoon lay on top of the beans. Huh, Kira thought, a potential tool or weapon? She picked up the spoon, heavier and softer than she expected. She bent it with a little effort. She dug it into the scrambled eggs and lifted. The spoon was stiff enough to hold light food but wouldn't crack and splinter as regular plastic cutlery might. It wasn't suitable as a stabbing weapon, though, Kira thought.

Kira chewed her food slowly, hoping there were no drugs in it. She wondered at herself, at how easily she could slip into the mind of a vicious attacker. Selena was probably like Rosa, except with more responsibility. This was just a job to her. Kira imagined Selena as a single mother raising three young children on her own. She knew she could not hurt Selena, unless she was fighting for her life. But wasn't she fighting for her life, her old life of freedom to come and go? Hadn't she felt her will to live, her life, slipping away in the aquarium?

Could she really take Selena on if she wanted to? Her new caretaker was built like a wrestler, all muscle, and maybe trained in martial arts and self-defence. Kira needed to move more, exercise, try to stay fit as long as she had the space and time to do it. However, the heat was oppressive in her small cabin. She glanced up at the ceiling, searching for vents where air should be moving in and out. She found two grates at opposite ends of the room. Reaching up, she could barely feel warm air passing through one of them. She felt nothing from the other one—probably a return vent. Lovely, she thought sarcastically. Here she was so close to the equator, and she found herself in a heated cell in the bowels of a cargo ship. Here was something else to discuss with Selena when she returned.

There was a knock on the door. Selena opened it a crack and then entered when she saw Kira sitting on her bed. She held two large bottles of water in one arm and closed the door with her other hand. She set the bottles on the shelf.

"I will bring tea this afternoon," she said, picking up the plate and turning for the door.

"Uh, Selena, do you know where I'm going?"

Selena stopped, her hand on the door handle, and gave a small smile. "No, I do not know."

"So, where does this ship go?"

"This ship? We go from the Caribbean coast of Panama to the Pacific coast, and then we return. Every day the same."

Kira thought she detected a slight roll of the eyes. "Wow, that must get boring. Day after day."

"Oh, you know, it is a good job. Finding work is not so easy here."

"So, I guess I'm going to the Pacific coast at least. And then being transferred?"

"I do not know. That is not my business." Selena had dropped her smile.

"Selena, do you get many passengers like me, who are locked in their little cabins?"

She frowned. "Sometimes."

"Do you know that I've been kidnapped? That you are involved in human trafficking?" Kira assumed that this woman did not know what she really was doing.

Selena's mouth dropped open. "No! That is not true! They said you might lie and say crazy things. You are not well."

Kira wanted to scream with laughter, but she clapped her hand over her mouth. So that's what they were told.

Selena began to turn the handle.

"Selena, please! Doesn't it seem strange to you? Psychiatric patients would be moved by medical people in medical transport, like ambulances, not put in cages like animals."

"This is not a cage—"

"It may as well be. I'm locked in. I can't come and go. They're probably going to drug me unconscious to move me again."

Selena's eyes were wide as she opened the door to leave.

"I'm from Canada. I want to go back home to my family! Selena, I'm not crazy—"

The door shut and locked. Kira may have put doubts into Selena's mind, but the woman would be too frightened to help and risk losing her good job. If she believed half of what Kira told her and had half a conscience, Selena's job just became even bleaker than it already was.

Kira groaned and fell back on the cot. She didn't even get to complain about the pathetic ventilation.

Chapter 13 –
The Laboratory

POOR VENTILATION was the least of Kira's problems. The tea was never delivered, and there were no more meals that day. Kira gave up the idea of getting any exercise. Overheated, she lay sprawled on her cot, sleeping fitfully and waking frequently from a series of nightmares. In one scenario, she and her dolphin friends were crammed together in a concrete pool and taught to perform tricks for fish. When she protested, the human trainers could not understand what she said. In another, she was unable to jump out of the water because her tail fin was missing, as if it had been amputated. Kira awoke sobbing.

She was awake when she heard the door opening in the blackness of night. There was no knock, no talking. Two large men hauled her off the cot and tied her hands behind her back. They grabbed each of her arms and led her out, gripping so tightly she dared not speak. They walked her along stuffy, tight corridors and up several flights of stairs until they emerged outside. The ship was docked at a typical port with a number of low flat-topped buildings surrounded by a chain-link fence. Kira was led down a ramp to a floating platform and then onto a small motorboat. They pushed her into the tiny head and shut the door. Now she was locked in a toilet. Shaking, her hands still tied, she sat on the seat and listened.

The voices were all Hispanic and too muffled for her to understand a word. The motor roared, and the boat heaved. Before long, they were rocking over waves. They had reached the open water of the Pacific Ocean. Without the use of her arms, Kira braced her legs against the walls to keep herself from sliding and banging into them.

For once she was glad to be confined in such a small space. Nearly an hour passed before the boat slowed and Kira heard shouting up top.

Her transporters opened the head door and led her out on the deck. The motorboat was moored near a much larger vessel. Kira's feet were tied together, and she was wrapped in a harness. A large hook was lowered down from the big boat and was attached to the harness. As she swung up into the air, the men in the small craft laughed and clapped. Kira seethed with anger. Greedy humans would fish for anything that brought them money, no matter the cost to others or to the planet.

Once on the deck of the larger boat, Kira was unwrapped and untied like a parcel and delivered to the bottom of the vessel. Her new accommodation was similar to the cabin on the Panamanian cargo ship, minus a window. She was now below the waterline. At this point, she would have welcomed some form of unconsciousness, as long as it didn't include any dreams.

Kira's keepers did not speak to her. They kept their distance, caring for her like an unpredictable exotic pet. They did not appear to fear her as they might a viper or a rare white tiger, but they were wary. Her voice would have no influence here, so she remained silent.

She lost track of time and had no idea how many days they had been travelling when she was finally led out of her cabin. In the dead of night, she was folded into the back seat of a car. Her arms and legs were free, but a Plexiglas shield separated her from the front seat. The car windows were tinted grey so no one could see inside, and she could barely see out. Kira sensed that they were driving through rolling hills, not unlike the swells traversed via a ship. When the car eventually slowed to a stop, Kira could make out a tall gate sliding open before they moved forward again. Turning around, she watched the gate slide closed behind them. Her new prison. Once out of the car, she was led into a darkened building and locked into another small, windowless room with a single bed.

Kira could not sleep. She sensed that this was her final stop. She wished there were a way to shut off her brain so that there would be no feeling, no memories, no anticipation, no fear, no nothing.

Clutching her Pendright, she finally drifted into a dream world. She found herself looking up at a blindingly blue sky and rocking gently side to side as if suspended in a hammock. However, the floor was hard, and on either side of her, the walls curved up. She lifted her head and saw a man rowing at the stern of the boat she lay in. She sat up and tried to make out his fuzzy features—a young man with a reddish beard. Was it Janus? Kira squinted at him, and he smiled at her. The sun glinted off his teeth. "Cody? Is that you?" As soon as she spoke, the smile evaporated, and a dark-green muzzle protruded from his face. He opened his jaws and chattered his triangular metallic teeth.

Kira's eyes popped open. She was staring at a blue ceiling. The room was lit by small sconces on all four walls. She heard a hum but couldn't tell if it came from the light fixtures. Looking around the room, she could see no switches for the lights.

Kira sat up. In spite of the comfortable mattress, she felt stiff, as if she'd been sleeping in a wooden rowboat. She stood up and stretched and then rubbed her arms and legs. She'd been confined too long, and soon all her muscles would atrophy from a lack of movement. What did it matter? She was already wasting away. If she stopped accepting all food now, the end would simply come sooner. She suddenly felt woozy and sat on the edge of her bed.

A clattering noise outside the door made her tense. It was the same noise that the beastly boatman had made in her dream. Someone knocked on the door. Kira did not answer. At the second knock, she heard a woman's voice.

"Hello? May I come in?"

Kira remained silent. She was afraid to open her mouth, unsure what sound might emerge.

The door opened slowly. A young woman peeked around the corner and then carefully stepped inside and closed the door. She wore a pale-green lab coat, one breast pocket full of pens and the other with a black clip attached. Her long blond hair was tied in a ponytail. She looked far too young to be a medical doctor.

"Good morning. My name is Sarah. I hope you had a good trip." She paused, waiting for Kira to speak.

Kira's mouth dropped open. Was she kidding? Kira closed her mouth firmly and stared at her.

"Okay, I guess you're probably a little disoriented. We're at the International Marine Mammal Institute. We call it 'IMMI' around here. I'm a graduate student doing a dissertation on exotic and rare marine mammals. My specialty is marine ethology. That's the study of behaviour—"

"I don't care!" Kira's voice burst out of her, surprising both of them. "I want to know why I am here and when I can leave." She wanted to stand up and face this woman, but she was afraid she'd fall over. She could feel her face burning.

Sarah put her hands up in front of her. "Okay, okay, stay calm. Look, I'm just a student here. I get that you didn't volunteer to help us with our studies." She shook her head and put her index finger over her lips to signal quiet. "I know this isn't conventional science, but the researchers who know about your kind are trying to keep it from the general public. I mean, if the word got out, all sorts of people would be trying to hunt you down for all sorts of nefarious purposes, you know, like selling you to secret illegal aquariums. Who knows what other horrible, degrading things they might do."

"You mean like what you're doing—capturing and using me for science?"

"Look, we didn't capture you. We have trusted people out there looking for the ones already captured, and we pay good money to get them out and to our facility, where it's safe. We'll do some simple testing, nothing that will harm you, and then send you home."

Kira's mouth dropped open. There were other study "subjects" like herself! She sputtered, "W-well why can't you just send us home right away?"

"I wish I could, but it's not my call. These government scientists are powerful, and they have a lot of resources and money. I don't agree with everything they do. In fact, when I signed up, I didn't realize our subjects weren't volunteers. I had stars in my eyes. I thought, 'Wow, I have a chance to study marine humanoid life. It's a dream come true!'" She paused when Kira's jaw dropped open again.

"Look, you'll just have to trust me. I'm on your side. Our staff are committed to making sure you are comfortable while you're here, and I'll personally see that this happens. I promise you will get back home safely."

Kira stared at Sarah, who was perhaps only a few years older than herself. She acted sincere, but Kira did not trust her. She would prefer to speak to the people in charge, the scientists responsible for this laboratory. For now, she'd play along.

"So," Sarah began again, "what is your name?"

"Coralene."

"That's pretty. Do you have a last name?"

"Not really. We marine humanoids usually go by one name." Kira did not plan to provide any scientists with information that would actually be useful to them—only enough to secure her release, if indeed that were a real possibility.

Sarah sighed and turned for the door. "Okay, we can do the intake paperwork later. How about some breakfast? Anything in particular you'd like to eat?"

Kira automatically put her hand on her growling stomach. "Yeah. I'd love some bacon and eggs," she said, challenging Sarah with the expectation of being turned down.

"Eggs and bacon, it will be. Scrambled, poached, sunny side up?" Sarah responded like a waitress taking a regular order. She did not react to Kira's look of surprise.

"Scrambled, please," Kira said automatically, realizing that she had slipped back into civility. She didn't have to be polite to anyone while she was still a prisoner. Sarah could never be treated as a friend. Then again, if there were any chance that they might release her, Kira should at least pretend to be cooperative.

Sarah returned with bacon and scrambled eggs as promised, along with a toasted bagel, a small pot of raspberry jam, and a cup of orange juice. "I forgot to ask if you'd like anything else to drink, besides the juice."

Kira was savouring the taste and texture of egg on toast. She swallowed and nodded. "Yeah, some water and herbal tea, no sugar or milk."

"Sure. I'll be right back. Then we can get started on the paperwork."

Kira continued to eat and drink slowly. So much for starving herself, she thought. She'd reassess once she saw what sort of testing they planned to do.

Sarah returned with a bottle of water and a tall paper cup of steaming tea. She stepped outside and then almost immediately walked back in with a chair and a clipboard. Kira sipped the peppermint tea and watched Sarah sit across from her and flip through several pages.

"Here we are. I just have a few questions before we take some measurements."

"Measurements?"

"Yes. Things like height and weight, length of limbs—you know, shoulder to elbow to wrist, length of digits, hip circumference, body temperature, and so on."

Kira gave her approximate age and made up a birth date. She made up a life history as well, telling Sarah that she mostly lived underwater and only emerged on land for short periods of time to learn about humans. She was fascinated by their homes, their diets, and daily rituals. Kira described her family of two loving parents and a younger brother and sister who frequently squabbled. She also threw in two aunts: one aunt with a nasty disposition, whom she patterned after Shree, and one very sweet aunt, whom she based on her real mother, Calista. Kira made up games that they played as youngsters, such as a version of underwater hide-and-seek. She spoke of young merrows helping to gather seaweed as garnishes for their fancier meals. Explaining their diet was the only information she provided that was almost completely truthful. Kira enjoyed recreating her life of make-believe. Sarah wrote furiously, occasionally interrupting with questions.

"So, did you have any boyfriends, Coralene?"

Kira frowned, pretending to be upset. She thought of Janus and described him to Sarah. "He was new to our area, just passing through I guess, but he seemed to like me, and, well, he left eventually. My parents never liked him, though."

"Do you know where he came from?"

"No, he was vague about his home. I guess that made my parents suspicious. My brother didn't like him, either."

"So, your brother was a bit protective of you?"

"I suppose."

"And where is your home area, Coralene?"

Kira raised her eyebrows. "I thought you were studying merrow behaviour. Why do you want to know where I come from?"

"Well, we believe that merrows are distributed throughout the world's oceans and that, like humans, they may have distinguishing features and behavioural characteristics, different cultures, depending on their genetic makeup and where they live. It's just data gathering."

"Can you tell me where this institute is located?" Kira asked.

"If I told you, would you tell me where you live?"

"That sounds fair," Kira said, without any intention of telling the truth.

"We're in California, just north of San Diego," Sarah said.

Kira swallowed. That was approximately where she thought they were, based on how long the trip from Panama had taken. Sarah should have lied if they planned to release her, in case Kira intended to inform the authorities about the institute's irregular and probably illegal activities. However, perhaps Sarah believed that Kira would not say anything, knowing that she would reveal the existence of merrows if she did. Or, more likely, they wouldn't believe her story and think she was deluded.

"My home is just south of Boston," Kira said. That wasn't true, but it was in the Atlantic. Kira hoped there were no merrow colonies in that area, but she didn't actually know. She wished she'd chosen a location farther from home.

"Okay, great. I think that's enough for now. Let's go take some measurements."

Sarah led her to a suite of rooms that reminded her of a science laboratory. A variety of instruments hummed around her, some on stainless steel counters, some on the floor. There were two refrigerators and two chest freezers, weighing balances, and a benchtop centrifuge, which Kira thought might be used to analyze blood.

"IMMI has state-of-the-art equipment here, the best that money can buy," Sarah said as they passed from lab to lab. They had stopped in front of what appeared to be a large round walk-in chamber surrounded by tinted glass, like the windows of the car that had delivered her.

"This biometric scanner is amazing," Sarah explained. "You walk in and stand still for about thirty seconds, and in that time, it will take all the measurements we need. You'll be weighed and scanned, and all your dimensions will be recorded electronically. We'll have a 3-D photo of you that we can store, and we're all done."

While she was talking, another green-coated employee had joined them. He had cropped grey hair, and he stood with his arms crossed, frowning. His name tag read "Jeff."

Kira shook her head. "I don't like the idea of going in there. How is the photo being taken? I know about X-rays. Is that what it is?" She had heard about full-body scanners at airports, and she was familiar with CAT scans and NMR technology; however, she did not want to let on that she knew that much.

Jeff spoke up. "It uses a type of long-wavelength energy that passes through your body. It's really cool. We've all had it done, and we're all fine. It's not new technology, though the computational algorithm is more advanced than most current models used commercially. It's perfectly safe." He sounded bored and exasperated at the same time.

"If it's so safe, I want to see someone else go in first," Kira insisted.

Jeff rolled his eyes. "I don't have time for this."

"I'm not going in."

Sarah raised her hand before Jeff could object. "Okay, Coralene. I'll go in. You watch Jeff run the computer, that instrument on the counter, and you'll see what happens. Go on. It'll be okay."

Kira followed Jeff to the computer and watched as Sarah took off her lab coat and stepped into the chamber. Jeff, shaking his head, punched at a keyboard, and Kira focused on the screen. The chamber door slid closed, and a light that shone down on Sarah encompassed her in a blood-red cocoon. Kira read *scanning* on the computer monitor and watched as a blue bar moved from left to right across the screen. The computer whined as another bar, this one green, moved across after the blue one. A few clicks later, the words *scan complete* flashed up, and the chamber door slid open. Sarah stepped out and opened her arms wide.

"See? No big deal."

Kira thought for a moment. "Why can't you take the measurements the old-fashioned way?"

"Because this is so much more efficient, and it takes measurements we can't do with a tape measure and weighing scale."

"Like what?"

"Well, like blood type and number of chromosomes, a genetic profile. You don't want us to take blood samples with a needle, do you?"

"No, I don't want you to take any blood or do genetic testing at all!" Kira was alarmed. Why did they want that information?

"Oh, for heaven's sake!" Jeff said. "You don't have a choice. In you go!" He grabbed Kira's arm and dragged her to the chamber.

"Jeff! Stop!" Sarah shouted at him. "If she struggles, we don't get clean measurements. Let her go."

Jeff released his hold and walked away to a far counter, his back turned to them.

"I'm really sorry, Coralene, but the project manager insists we get the data this way. It really is harmless. We won't use the data to hurt you or any other merrows. It's purely academic research. They want to understand how merrows are different from humans. We study human biometrics the same way, and that information helps us with understanding disease conditions and treating sick people, sometimes with gene therapy. It's possible they could use it to help merrows in the future. But for now, it's just being collected and stored."

Kira was not happy, but she believed they would get the data from her eventually, by force if they had to. She nodded and stepped into the chamber. When the door slid closed, she shuddered and closed her eyes. It's only for thirty seconds, she told herself. At the sound of a click, she began to chant in her head. One thousand and one, one thousand and two, she counted. She abruptly stopped; her concentration shattered by a loud screech and a blaring siren. The door slid open to the sound of people shouting.

"Get out of there! Get out, Coralene!" Sarah was reaching for her as Kira jumped out of the chamber. "Are you okay?"

Kira nodded. Stunned, she put her hand on her chest as if she were clutching at her heart. She felt the Pendright, hot beneath her hand, but she did not dare look down under her shirt. It was probably glowing an angry orange. She did not want them to try to take it from her.

As Sarah led her out of the laboratory and back to her room, she apologized for the equipment malfunction, admitting she had no idea of what had gone wrong. She assured Kira that their technicians would figure it out.

Kira had one strong image in her head. "Sarah, I need to be in the water. Can I do that here?"

"Uh, sure. I was going to take you there tomorrow, but I guess we can go now. Is that what you want to do? You're not feeling well?"

"No, something's wrong. I need to be in water. It's an instinct kind of thing." She hoped that was convincing enough for the ethology graduate student.

"Okay. I'll take you to the merrow gardens right away. I think you'll like it there. We've spent a lot of time and money to make it as natural as possible. You'll feel right at home."

Chapter 14 –
Merrow Gardens

KIRA COULDN'T WAIT to see these gardens that Sarah was so certain she'd love. The idealistic young student had no inkling that her treatment of Kira was so degrading. To her, Kira was a specimen to be evaluated and reduced to computer algorithms and statistics. What kind of underwater dollhouse had her mad-scientist masters built for the merrows they wished to study?

Kira's anxiety grew as they walked briskly along hallways, down a long set of stairs, and then through a tunnel that apparently connected separate buildings. What if she were going to be thrown into another tank with artificial plants and paintings on the walls? Still, she couldn't wait to slip into soothing water. Her Pendright continued to exude heat, like a flat iron stuck to her chest. She wondered if it had now actually adhered to her skin, as it did underwater.

At the end of the tunnel, they climbed up two flights of stairs. Kira gasped when they opened a door into a huge, brightly lit room. She looked up. They were in a giant solarium, with glass reaching at least two stories high and curving over them. At the base, rising about eight feet, the glass was an opaque grass green. The room held several small tables and comfortable lounge chairs arranged around a shallow oval pool in the centre. Surely, this wasn't a merrow garden? Looking over as they passed by, Kira noticed a few orange and black koi swimming in the pool.

Sarah turned around and laughed at Kira's expression. "We're not there yet. This is an informal meeting room for small groups. Sometimes we have seminars in here, but not if we need to project slides or videos. It's too bright."

As they approached the wall straight ahead of them, Kira noticed that it reached about fifteen feet high and that clear glass extended straight up to the glass ceiling. "They sure used a lot of glass to build this place," she muttered.

"It's a special type of clear polymer that's virtually indestructible. It bends easily, so it's much easier to work with than even thin Plexiglas." Sarah opened a door, and they walked into a room with an enormous pool. She put her arm out to block Kira, who was veering toward it, as if pulled by a magnet.

"This isn't your merrow garden yet, and don't get any closer. There's an invisible energy barrier around it that won't allow us through."

Kira stopped. "What kind of energy? What happens if I touch it?"

"I'll show you." Sarah removed a pen from her pocket and threw it toward the pool. In mid-air, about three feet from the edge of the pool, the pen bounced back and fell, as if it had hit a solid wall. Sarah picked it up. "That's what happens."

Aha, an invisible barrier for their captive subjects, Kira thought. "So, have you tested it yourself? Like the biometric chamber?"

Sarah smiled. "As a matter of fact, I have. All the staff here are required to touch it at least once so they understand how it works and why we should avoid running into it. It's like static shock, not terrible, but not pleasant either. You ever been shocked, Coralene?"

Kira nodded. "And I don't need to test the barrier, if it's okay with you. One shock was enough for me today."

"Oh? I didn't know you got shocked in the chamber. Maybe our medical staff should check you out?"

"No, I didn't mean an electric shock. I mean the mental kind. The whole experience was, well, unnerving."

"Oh, I'm sure it was horrible. We've never had that happen before. I'm really sorry. I'm sure the techs will figure out what went wrong."

They walked past the large pool, opened another door into a second pool room and then a third, where they stopped. Sarah gave Kira a huge smile and waved her hand at the water. "This will be your home for a while, Coralene. I hope you'll have everything you need here. The barrier is down now so you can go in, but once you're in the pool, the barrier will be turned on for your own safety. No one without approval will be allowed in or out."

When she spoke about the barrier, Sarah glanced back at the door they had just entered. There was a black panel on the wall to the right of the door. A faint green light blinked in the top left corner.

"If you need anything or want to speak to me, there's an intercom on the floor at the edge of the pool here, as well as at the other end." She walked to the nearest corner and pointed out the speaker. "And if we want to get your attention, we can buzz you and talk to you through the intercom. The sound can also be transmitted underwater."

Kira was anxious to jump in. "Is the pool stocked with food?" she asked.

"Of course. If you have any special requests for types of fish or greens, just let me know. Give me a buzz. If I can't return any of your calls right away, they'll be recorded. Just like an answering machine, if you know what that is."

Kira nodded and tried not to smile. "I've heard of them."

"Anything else?"

"No." Kira had moved to the edge and was ready to jump.

"Make yourself at home—"

Kira heard no more. She was underwater and swimming fast for the centre and bottom of the pool. The Pendright glowed blue green for a moment and was no longer hot. Relieved, Kira sank to the sandy bottom, amidst thick bunches of seagrasses. She didn't know whether Sarah was watching her from above or whether there were cameras monitoring her movements. She covered the Pendright with her hands until the glow had faded completely and once again blended in with her scales.

Above water, she looked around at her new home. It was the size of an Olympic-sized swimming pool, with at least fifteen feet of decking on all four sides. Below the surface, if she pretended she was not surrounded by walls, she could easily be at the bottom of the ocean somewhere off California. She pushed off to explore the rest of the garden. The floor was covered with charcoal-coloured sand and a number of large grey boulders. The varieties of seaweed were not exactly the same as those found in the northern Atlantic, but they were not that different, either. She watched as fish swam by, some species recognizable, others not. She thought she could probably name most of them. Cody would have been able to name them all, as well as the plants. What she wouldn't give for the sight of his friendly, happy, goofy face. That's what this place was missing: companions. Although it appeared to be natural, this was indeed a prison, not home.

Kira snacked on a couple of small fish, but she wasn't particularly hungry after her huge breakfast. As she continued to swim, she studied the entire garden enclosure, gradually becoming familiar with every rock and the distribution of seagrasses. There was no place she could hide completely from above. She pushed on a few boulders and found she could shift them slightly as they slid on the layer of sand, thousands of tiny ball bearings on the slick concrete floor below. Kira wondered if there might be a hidden floor drain somewhere. She located the intake and outtake grates on opposite walls that provided a fresh stream of seawater flowing through the pool. She could actually drift on the current it created, and swimming against it provided a nice physical workout. This was how she planned to stay fit and strong. Kira was determined to escape this prison, no matter how pleasant the scientists had made it.

She took a short nap after burning up her nervous energy. When she awoke, she swam to the top and listened. In addition to the occasional sound of water slapping against the sides, a soft droning filled the air. Maybe this unfamiliar sound was being emitted from the shock barrier or the ceiling ventilation system, she thought. She then swam to the end of the pool where she had first entered the water. After pushing herself up and onto the deck, Kira stood up slowly and held her arm out toward the barrier. She looked down at the Pendright. It glowed softly as she took a step forward but gave off no warmth. She continued to move forward, two then three feet. The Pendright flashed purple, but there was no shock, no unusual sound. The green light in the black panel continued to blink. She took another step and then yet another. She was at least six feet beyond the edge of the pool. No alarms went off that she could hear.

Kira walked up to the panel. She could see the switch for turning the barrier on and off. She tried to open the door next to the panel, but it was locked. She turned around and walked to the door on the other side, but it was also locked. Kira turned back toward the pool, prepared for a shock, but she passed through the barrier again with only a brief purple pulse from her Pendright. She dove into the pool and waited. No one came; nothing happened. All was silent underwater.

Kira had fallen asleep and was awakened by a buzz that vibrated through the water. When her eyes opened, the water around her was much darker. She slowly moved up to the surface, noticing the soft light from lamps lining the walls of the room. Sarah stood just outside the energy barrier. She raised her arm when she saw Kira.

"Hello, Coralene!" she shouted, louder than she needed for Kira to hear. "I'm just checking to see how you're doing before I head back."

Head back where, Kira wondered. Did she live outside the fences that surrounded the institute? Or in a student dormitory?

"Are you okay? Did you eat?"

Kira swam closer. "Yes, I'm okay. I ate a little."

"Oh good. And I wanted to let you know that we got a few of your measurements from the scanner after all. Mostly morphometrics. We can do blood work another time for the rest of the data. Some of the numbers are a little different from others we've taken, but I think they'll be useable."

Kira perked up. "What other numbers?"

"Oh, from other merrows."

Kira's heart raced. "Are they here now? Other merrows?" Was it possible that some of her friends had also been captured during the Spegar attack? Janus or Borin?

Sarah did not say anything for a moment. She looked briefly at the door. "There are one or two."

"You don't know how many?"

"Well, one for sure. The other one is a little different. Actually, they're both different from you, from different areas. That's one of the things we're interested in studying, some of the physical differences between groups or races." Sarah shifted on her feet. She seemed uncomfortable.

"Will I get a chance to meet them?" Kira felt breathless. Even if she didn't know them, she wanted to learn more about this facility and what was really going on. "I'd love to meet different merrows. I only got to know my family and the local merrows back home. Maybe they don't even speak the same language." She shuddered, hoping neither was a Spegar.

"So far we can only speak to one of them. The other one won't come out of the water."

Sarah had not answered Kira's question. "Since you're interested in studying merrow behaviour, wouldn't you like to learn how we interact with each other, too?"

"Perhaps. But I have a protocol to follow for this study before I could add any new variables. I'd have to discuss it with my supervisor."

Kira shook her head. "The one thing that is missing from this lovely garden is company. We merrows live in groups like humans. We can get lonely and depressed, like you." Kira stared hard at Sarah, whose eyes had grown wide. She continued. "You're not studying normal merrow behaviour at all. You're looking at the effects of captivity and depression on merrows without knowing how healthy, normal merrows behave." Kira slapped the surface of the water with her tail.

Sarah's mouth dropped open. Kira wondered if she'd said too much.

"Well, okay, I guess that's a valid point. Actually, there's a new researcher being added to my thesis committee. It might be something he'd be interested in. Anyway, I have to go. See you in the morning," she said and hurried out.

Kira swam fast-paced loops around and through the pool, excited by the prospect of meeting other merrows. She tried to stay calm and not to build up her hopes. She hadn't realized how lonely she was, how much she yearned for real companionship. Up to now, she had been focused on escape, and that was a goal she would never let go of. However, if she could talk to another merrow who had been here longer, she might acquire the information she needed to find a way out...or she might not.

Chapter 15 –
In the Name of Science

THE NEXT FEW DAYS were filled with frequent visits from Sarah and endless questionnaires. Kira continued to pester her about meeting the other merrows until Sarah finally gave in. She promised to arrange a visit if Kira cooperated and answered all the questions. She was looking for exact, minute details of Kira's family, their physical traits, behaviour, and health histories. As she had done earlier, Kira fabricated much of the information, with a few real facts thrown in.

Sarah was particularly interested in any merrow history or lore that had been passed down. Kira did not know a great deal, except for what Calista and Currin had shared with her in the past few years. She had grown up as a human, not a mermaid, so she had to create an entire undersea childhood. She worried that if Sarah found out she'd been raised in a land-based community, they might never let her go.

Less pleasant than the questionnaires were the underwater measurements. For these, Sarah donned scuba gear and was accompanied by Henry, a tall, muscular diver. One other technical assistant, Wally, remained on the pool deck and entered data into a handheld computer. Sarah and Henry wore fancy diving helmets with speakers and microphones and full face masks, whereas Wally, positioned safely on deck, wore only headphones.

Kira was mildly amused by some of the data they collected. Intrigued by her tail, they took every conceivable measurement, including the number of fin spines and their thickness, length, circumference, and spacing. Every step was photographed. They also videoed her swimming back and forth and her jumping out of the pool and back in again, fascinated with each transformation. She remembered how awestruck she was the first time she dove into the sea and discovered her morphed body.

They, of course, noticed her Pendright when she swam underwater. When they questioned her about it, she said she had been born with it, that it was part of her scale structure. They had obviously seen other merrows who did not have such an adornment. Kira deliberately misinformed them that about half the merrows in her colony had them. She'd also heard that merrows off the coast of Africa had unusual scale patterns on their chests and around their necks. When she was out of the water, she was grateful for the high collar on her blue coveralls, which hid the loose Pendright. She was certain they would have removed it if they could, though unknowingly at their own peril. Kira smiled, thinking of the electrified kidnapper who had unwisely touched it, not to mention anyone else who may have attempted to handle it while she was sedated.

They were still keen to get her genetic profile to compare to the others they had collected. So far, she had resisted giving them any blood. Once they had finished their physical measurements, she figured they would try to get that sample, one way or another.

When Sarah buzzed her the morning after the last questionnaire, Kira swam slowly, reluctantly to the surface. She was certain this would be the day. Would they try to drug her if she didn't let them take a blood sample? She didn't know why she was so resistant. Perhaps she was afraid they would not release her after the testing as Sarah had promised. Perhaps they had something even worse planned for her.

Sarah, however, was beaming at Kira as though she had just been nominated for a Nobel Prize. "Good morning, Coralene! I have some great news for you." She paused.

"Oh?" Kira did not feel as hopeful as Sarah probably thought she should.

"Yes. I got the go-ahead to let you spend some time with Maya today. She lives in one of the other gardens. We'll open a panel in between to let her through and then close it. You'll have about an hour to visit. How does that sound?" She continued to smile, pleased with her message.

Kira thought a moment before she spoke. "Thank you, Sarah. I really appreciate this." Sarah didn't mention any conditions. Would their meeting be recorded by video? As yet, she hadn't found any sign of camera or sound equipment underwater, so she thought this possibility not likely…unless Maya herself was wired.

She slipped back underwater and waited, watching the wall along its length. She'd found several places with seams in the concrete and wondered if they had been connected to other pools at one time.

Kira began to swim slowly along the wall. She was nervous. What if this merrow were a Spegar or from some other unfriendly clan? She suddenly felt terribly sad, wondering how long Maya had been in their clutches.

Not far from the top end of the pool, a dark square opening appeared in the wall. Kira positioned herself in front of it. Nothing happened for a minute. Then a head appeared, and Maya emerged in all her mermaid glory.

She was much longer than Kira, with most of the extra length made up by her tail. Her iridescent scales sparkled, and her elegant tail, looking as if it had been dipped in a bucket of rainbow paint, trailed behind her like the feathers of a tropical bird. Her wavy dark hair framed an oval face, pale in complexion. She smiled broadly, revealing long, even teeth.

"Greetings. I am Maya," she said, bowing her head. She then looked up again. "I am so happy to meet you!" She beat her tail so that her entire slim body undulated.

Kira smiled at her excitement. "I'm Coralene. Glad to meet you, too, Maya. Where are you from?"

"I come from near Dominica. In the Caribbean. And you, Coralene? Such a beautiful name for a mermaid."

Maya's accent and cadence reflected her exotic appearance, Kira thought. As if on cue, the two mermaids began to swim alongside each other.

"My father told me about the Caribbean merrows he met when he was a young man. He told me that he had never seen such beautiful mermaids anywhere else in his travels. Now that I've met you, I have to agree with him."

Maya's laugh tinkled like a bell. "You are well brought up, young Coralene." She stopped suddenly and pointed at Kira's chest. "I remember a story about merrows coming from the north. One had an unusual ornament such as yours. Was he one of your people, perhaps?"

Kira wanted to shout, "That was my father!" but she clamped her lips shut for a moment. "Perhaps. There are a number of us with this pattern. It may be African. I don't know."

Maya cocked her head and smiled. "Mm-hmm. Have you ever met any African merrows?"

"No. Have you?"

"No, but I hear they have long tails like us. Maybe not so colourful. These differences are interesting, are they not?"

Kira nodded, wondering how much Maya really knew. However, she didn't dare stray from the story she'd told Sarah. She had no way of knowing what kind of relationship this mermaid had with Sarah. Maybe Maya had been instructed to extract more personal details from her. Maybe that was why Sarah had decided to let them spend time together.

"So, Maya, how long have you been here?" she asked.

"Ahh, I do not know for certain. Too long, I think."

"A week, a month, or longer?" Surely, she must have some idea, Kira thought.

"We do not measure time like humans. Do you?"

"I... I spent some time with humans. I liked to explore on land, so I learned a little about their customs. Measuring time by a clock can be useful on occasion."

Maya had stopped and drifted down to a large boulder. She draped herself over the rock as if it were a piece of cushy living room furniture. Kira settled on the sand below her. "I suppose we also measure time, but it is marked by seasons of the sea and the air above. Perhaps I have been here one season or even longer. Every day-night cycle is much like any other in the garden where I live."

"Have you ever been on land, Maya?"

"Only when they brought me to this place after the capture. I learned a lot about humans in a few day-night cycles." Maya had lowered her head so her hair covered her face, and Kira could not read her expression. "But here they have been kind to me. I know I will go home soon." She raised her head and gave Kira a weak smile.

"And you've been alone all this time? I heard there might be another merrow here also," Kira said.

"I do not know of any other merrows except for my daughter," Maya said.

"What? You have a daughter here?"

Maya laughed. "She came with me, but they released her back to our home. I promised to stay as long as they needed if they would let her go. She was so frightened when she saw her tail had split into two legs. And I was so angry."

"Did she walk?"

Maya shook her head and smiled. "She would not walk. She clung to me, and they had to carry us both. She would not eat. She was too upset. So they sent her back home to our clan."

Kira wondered if her daughter had really been returned to her home. Maya would have no way of knowing. Kira shivered. "Do you know when you'll be leaving?"

"Soon. The tests are nearly finished, I think. And you are here now." She flashed a toothy smile.

What did that mean? Was Kira a replacement for Maya? Or was Maya happy to have some company, if only for a short while? And what were all the tests that took a season or more? Kira was not at all as assured as Maya seemed to be.

They swam and chatted about their families, caught a few small fish to eat, and talked about the different species and foods found in their original homes. Maya described all the tests that Sarah and the other scientists had put her through, nothing too harrowing so far. Kira did not learn as much as she had hoped to from her neighbour.

The two merrows had stopped to rest on some boulders when Kira was startled by the warning buzz, indicating their time was up. Maya laughed. "You will get used to it, Coralene." She peeled herself off her boulder and swam closer to Kira. "Or should I say, 'Princess Coralene'?"

Kira frowned and shook her head.

"Do not worry. I will not tell them," she whispered and patted Kira's arm. "Be agreeable, and they will treat you well."

She turned away and glided back toward the tunnel, glittering as she swam. Watching the last of the rainbow tail disappear from view, Kira felt as though she'd been abandoned by a dear old friend. Would she ever see Maya again? She hoped so. She'd even donate some blood; she was that starved for friendly company.

Chapter 16 –
Dr. Giles Morton

THE NEXT MORNING, Kira floated up slowly, groggy after a listless night. She'd had unsettling dreams of sparkling young mermaids being caught in drift nets and hauled aboard filthy fishing trawlers. They were thrown into holding tanks with hundreds of fish, sharks, and squid. When a lid slammed down, Kira found herself thrashing inside the dark tank, struggling to evade the death grip of squid tentacles and to fight off sharks. She woke up screaming in a cloudy storm of stirred-up sand. It had taken some time for her heart to stop pounding and the water to clear.

As she approached the surface, Kira could see two people standing on the deck, both wearing pale-green IMMI lab coats. Sarah was accompanied by a bearded man in black-rimmed glasses. One of Sarah's supervisors, she supposed. Out of the water and without her own glasses, she could not clearly make out their facial features.

"Good morning, Coralene!" Sarah called out with her customary morning cheerfulness. "This is Dr. Giles Morton from the Haida Gwaii Aquatic Research Institute up in Canada. He's my new co-supervisor."

Kira waved her hand at him, not feeling particularly sociable. "Hi."

Dr. Morton nodded. "Good morning," he said.

"Dr. Morton is an exercise and behavioural physiologist. So he'll be taking a few different measurements in the water for some baseline values." Sarah turned to look at him. "And you want to start today, right?"

"That's correct. If Coralene doesn't mind?" He crossed his arms and then tugged on his sandy-coloured beard.

Kira's heart hammered so hard she could feel her Pendright pulsing. She squinted her eyes to see the scientist more clearly, but it didn't help. He reminded her of someone. Had she met this man before?

"It's okay," she murmured when she could speak.

"Great. Sarah, can you help me set up? We can begin taking measurements this afternoon."

"Uh, sure, Dr. Morton. But I have a seminar all afternoon and some prep work I still need to do. Wally can probably help you."

"That's fine, Sarah. Once everything is set up, it's recorded automatically."

"Really?"

"Absolutely. I can show you how it works another time, if you're interested."

"Sure. Thanks, Dr. Morton."

Kira watched them leave. Before Dr. Morton passed through the door, he looked back at Kira and gave a small nod, as if saying goodbye. He was very polite, she thought. She wondered if she should be worried about these new measurements.

She watched throughout the morning as Wally helped Dr. Morton set up his equipment on the deck. The tall apparatus had five screens arranged vertically, one above the other. When she got bored with their activities, she swam against the current and caught a few small fish to eat. She'd discovered a plant in the pool with small cocoa-coloured berries that reminded her of the loram puffs on the East Coast. The West Coast variety had a nuttier flavour, rather like walnuts. She'd eaten most of the berries and thought she might ask for more plants.

When Kira surfaced later that morning and heard Dr. Morton speaking, her heart skipped again. For a moment she pictured Cody. That voice reminded Kira of her best friend. Then she felt herself constrict, as if an invisible fist had punched her in the stomach. She missed Cody so much. Where was he now? What was he doing? Did he know she was missing? Did he think she was dead, as everyone else probably did?

Kira dove under again and cried and cried. She couldn't stop. Through half-opened eyes, she could see her tears being carried away on the current. They formed a stream of tiny clear spheres before they dissolved into the heavier seawater and disappeared. For some reason that made her smile and laugh. Cody would love to see that, and then he'd apologize for being insensitive. She would tell him one day, she promised herself. She would get out of here and tell him everything.

The next time Kira surfaced, they had all left. For lunch, she assumed. She sank to the bottom to take a nap, exhausted after her poor night of sleep and drained by all the morning drama.

A buzz awoke Kira, and she shot up to the surface. She felt refreshed now and more curious than anxious about what this scientist had in store for her. She was surprised to see him in a diving suit, sitting in a chair in front of the mysterious tower of screens. He finished typing on a keyboard and turned to look at her.

"Hello, Coralene. I'm going to get into the water with you, if you don't mind, and attach a couple of small monitors. It won't hurt at all. They will record metabolic gases, such as oxygen, carbon dioxide, and nitrogen. Basically, the gases we find in the atmosphere. Okay?"

Kira nodded. "Why are you measuring those gases?"

"I want to establish a baseline, what your body produces at rest. So you don't need to do anything. I'll fit you out with a diving helmet like I'll be wearing, but it has a special collar that will stick to your scales and keep the water out. Then we'll turn on the air to see if access to gases inside the helmet changes your metabolic output."

Kira thought about this. It had never occurred to her to use air underwater when she didn't need to breathe normally as humans did.

"You see," he continued, "we don't know what changes when your body is submerged. Do you even need air to function like other sea animals that extract oxygen from the water through structures like gills, for instance? I've never seen gills on merrows. If you need oxygen, how do you get it? Through your skin, through the tail fin?"

Kira felt dizzy. She wondered if she were dreaming. She was hearing Cody's voice. Those were questions he used to ask, things they both wondered about. She shook her head.

"You okay?" he asked.

"Yeah, I'm fine."

He stood up and attached his diving helmet to his suit. The air tank was a tiny cylinder of super-compressed gas attached to the top of the helmet. Dr. Morton slipped into the water beside Kira, placed the helmet over her head, and attached it to her shoulder scales. He sank beneath the surface and motioned at her to follow him. He checked that her helmet was not leaking and then pointed away from the deck. The scientist swam into the middle of the large pool with Kira behind him. She wondered why he hadn't stayed near his recording instruments. She kept some distance between them. He seemed harmless, but something wasn't quite right.

"Coralene, can you hear me?"

Kira stopped short, startled at the tinny voice in her helmet. He turned around to face her.

"Y-yes, I can hear you. And you can hear me, too?"

"I can. This way we can talk while I work. And no one else can hear us."

Kira tensed, prepared to swim to safety if she had to. What was he up to? This was getting weird.

"You don't recognize me, do you?"

"Uh, no." She felt her Pendright pulsing again. "Uh, you remind me of someone," she admitted, shivering.

"Maybe I remind you of Cody?" He laughed and spread his arms out wide. "Kira, it's me, Cody."

Kira had never fainted before, but for a moment she saw glittery dancing seahorses in the water around them. Was she hallucinating or about to pass out? Her eyes began to water, which sharply improved her vision. Through his helmet glass she could see Cody's toothy grin peeking out of that ridiculous beard.

He raised his right hand. She raised hers and swam toward him; they smacked their hands together in victory. Then he grasped both of her hands in his and put the face of his helmet against hers.

"We found you, Kira. We found you! We're getting you out of here."

Kira tried to hug him, but their bulging helmets made it awkward to reach around. She could only grasp his shoulders, which she suddenly realized were much more muscular than she had remembered.

She giggled. "Cody, you've been working out!"

"The inevitable result of constantly hauling heavy gear and equipment on the ship. I was the junior on board. I got all the grunt work."

"What? Not in the lab twenty-four seven?"

"Not quite. Listen, Kira. We've got a plan to get you out, but it will take a little time. You need to go along with me on the tests I set up for you."

"Whoa! Who is 'we'?" Kira fluttered around Cody; she could not stay still.

"I'll tell you. But first let's get these monitors attached, okay? So we'll collect that baseline data while we talk." Cody removed a flat rectangular box the size of a large watch and strapped it to Kira's right arm over her skin. Then he attached a smaller one to her left arm just below her shoulder and over the scales. Finally, he clipped a tiny round monitor over the inside edge of her tail fin.

"I'm going to swim back to the data screens so I can make sure the recording has started. You wait here and try not to move. I know you're excited to see me, but you'll have to remain calm. Can you do that?"

"Ha!" Kira retorted. She didn't see his expression as he swam off, but she could imagine the smirk on his face.

"Looks fine," he reported. "Swim back and forth a bit. Yeah, that's it. Wow, cool. It's working perfectly. I love this technology. We're going to get a patent for this baby."

"'We'? You keep saying 'we.' Who are 'we'?"

Cody swam up to Kira, still grinning. "Man, it's good to see you, Kira. You have no idea how hard it was to find you. We've sent word to your parents that we have eyes on you now."

"'We'?" Kira was growing highly impatient with all the secrecy.

"Yeah, 'we.' Lots of people have been looking for you. But quietly, so we didn't spook the guys that had you. Anyway, Borin is out there just off the coast. He's on a ship we borrowed from the research fleet, a smaller vessel than the one I was working on this summer."

"Borin? He's okay? Oh, thank Neptune." Kira clutched her hands together. She only just realized that in spite of their antagonistic history, she cared about her cousin more than she knew. And here he was, not far away, trying to rescue her. "What about the others? Who survived the Spegar attack?"

"There were some injuries, but only Elder Crane didn't make it. And Janus disappeared. They never found him. No body, no sign of him. Sorry."

Kira nodded, her lips pressed together. She was relieved that most of them had made it, that it wasn't the complete slaughter she'd feared.

"I don't know if this will make it any better for you, but Chris was pretty sure that Janus got away. He started to swim after you, but they lost track of him in the fight."

Kira nodded. "Janus is smart. He's experienced. He's been on his own so long. I bet he got away." She paused, picturing his escape and wondering why he hadn't stayed to fight. "So, if he's alive, why didn't he let the others know?"

Cody shrugged. "Did you know there are other merrows here?"

"Yes. I met Maya the other day. A Caribbean merrow. She's gorgeous, just as Currin described. She had a daughter with her, but Maya said she was returned to their home. Do you know if that's true?"

Cody's expression had become very serious. "I don't know. I saw Maya, and she is spectacular. I didn't talk to her. She just waved at me."

"She said she was going home soon. Can you find out if they're really going to release her?"

"I'll try. But honestly, I don't know if they're going to let me in on all their plans. I'm here mainly to take specific measurements and do physiology tests. And help Sarah with her thesis work. I'll see what I can find out, but I need to be careful about the questions I ask. I don't want them to get suspicious."

"I'm worried they won't release her, in case she causes trouble for them afterwards."

"Yeah, you may be right. Though she's from an area where the merrows don't interact with humans, so it's not likely she'd be turning these pseudoscientists in to the authorities. Anyway, they may have other plans for her."

Kira shot him a worried look.

"There is something else. I saw another mermaid, one that won't come out of the water or talk to anyone. They say she arrived a few weeks before you did. She has really long jet-black hair, small eyes, and different hands, more like claws. Remind you of anyone?"

"Oh no, not Shree?"

"I don't know why not. Borin says she was gone by the time you got to Merhaven to turf out the finfolk. Maybe she was captured the same way you were."

Kira did not know what to say. By now she knew anything was possible.

"By the way, I hear you've developed new talents since I last saw you, Kira. Or should I address you as 'Princess Lance-a-Lot'? Okay, okay, I'll stop teasing. You are handy with a spear after all. Congrats on taking out a finfolk."

Kira narrowed her eyes and couldn't help sticking her tongue out at him, though she jammed it against the glass. Oh, how she had missed all his ribbing and puns.

"I wonder if they'd let me have an audience with the former Queen Shree. Maybe I could get her to talk. Would they let me have a spear, do you think?" She snorted, imagining such a meeting. "Lemon juice might not work underwater," she added, referring to an effective finfolk deterrent on land.

"Actually, they might let you have that audience. They're dying to know more about her type of 'merrow.' We know she can't talk out of water. Do you think she'd talk to you?"

Kira considered this for a moment. "I don't know. She might think it was hilarious to see me here. Maybe we could trade abduction stories. I could update her on how her children are doing, but she probably wouldn't care about them. Who knows."

"I'll see if it's possible. But you'd probably need something to protect yourself, and I doubt they'd let you have a weapon."

Kira laughed. "I won't need a weapon. I'll stay close to the deck. I'm fast and a great jumper. Next time I see Cass, I'm going to challenge him to a jumping competition. Anyway, I could get out of the water. And if it is Shree, or some other finfolk, she'd have a hard time once she was on the deck, if she got that far. Then I could run through the force field if I had to."

"You can?"

Kira pointed to her Pendright. "My special scale ornamentation. Currin gave it to me. On land, it's like a pendant, loose around my neck. If anyone tries to touch it, they get a shock. And it crashes their scanner and lets me through their invisible barrier. In the water, it attaches to my scales. Cool, huh?"

Cody's eyes had grown large. "Yeah, very cool. I'd love to figure out how it works, but I'll have to leave that for another time. Right now, you'd better start moving so I have results to show for our time underwater."

"Yessir!" Kira saluted him.

For the next hour, Kira swam laps of the pool at different speeds with the helmet on and no additional air, then with air, and finally with the helmet off, au naturel. She was thrilled to swim hard and fast, knowing that her best friend was in the pool with her and that he had a plan to spring her out of prison. She could not remember ever feeling this happy. At the same time, she pulled a small drag of doubt behind her, worried that Cody might be found out before she could escape. She knew only too well that anything could happen, good or bad.

Chapter 17 – Old Nemesis

SARAH SEEMED IMPRESSED with Dr. Morton's test results. At his bidding, Kira demonstrated her underwater prowess with heavy objects compared to her weaker strength on land. Apparently, the institute had only tested a handful of merrows to date and were still learning much about their abilities.

While underwater, Cody privately told Kira that he planned to run tests with her in the water off the Pacific coast. IMMI owned a corralled part of a rocky beach where, years ago, California sea lions had been kept for the benefit of tourists. Before they could proceed, he needed to convince the directors of two things: first, that there was a good reason for performance testing outside of the relatively small pools inside their facility and, second, that Kira would not be able to escape from that beach or the fenced-off inlet.

Cody also reported that Maya was no longer in the adjoining merrow garden. No one would tell him where she was or what had happened to her. "I told them I had been hoping to run a few tests with Maya to compare them with your results," he told Kira. "Everyone shrugs like they don't know anything and then move on. I had to stop asking before they got suspicious."

Two days later, Sarah spoke to Kira about the unusual merrow in one of their garden pools. "Dr. Morton seems to think you might be able to communicate with our dark, mysterious merrow. She can't—or simply won't—talk to us. Do you think you could?"

Kira tried not to smile. Dark and mysterious—what an appropriate way to describe the uncooperative merrow and Shree, if they were indeed one and the same. "I wouldn't mind trying. She might speak a different language, but I had no trouble understanding Maya."

"No, but Maya wasn't all that different from you. Our directors would really like to learn more about this one. And we'd have several people around in case there was any trouble. You know, ready to help out."

Kira gave a little laugh. "Oh, I think I'd be okay. I could jump out if I needed to get away."

"I'm sure you could, but we don't want to take any chances. Okay, I'll set it up."

Kira could hardly wait. Would it be her old nemesis? She could feel herself itching for a fight. She was still angry with Shree for imprisoning her royal parents for seventeen years and nearly destroying Merhaven.

She didn't have to wait long. Sarah, accompanied by Dr. Morton, Henry, and Wally, arrived the very next day to invite Kira out of the pool and on a field trip down the hall. Wally wore his lab coat and had a video camera hanging around his neck. The others wore their diving suits, and Henry carried an aquatic stun gun in a holster strapped to his waist. They walked into the room next door, where Kira thought Maya may have been staying, out the other side, and then along a long corridor. The next door they opened led into a smaller merrow garden.

Kira noticed a faint, peculiar odour right away. She remembered it well: the nauseating stench of adult finfolk up close. In this room, there was only the mere hint of finfolk musk, however.

She said nothing as they walked around the pool, looking for the dark merrow. She was lounging on the bottom, near the centre of the garden. Kira could not make out the features, but the shape was certainly that of a merrow. She had never heard Sarah say anything about finfolk, and she wondered if they were aware of these creatures.

"Okay, I'm ready," Kira said and then swallowed. She tried not to think of the poisonous claws and the knife-like teeth of finfolk in their natural forms.

The others took up positions on all four sides of the pool. Wally began to record. As Kira prepared to dive in, Henry and Cody snapped on their diving helmets and slipped into the water at opposite ends of the pool. They sank to the bottom and waited.

Kira dove in and slowly approached the figure in the middle. When she was more than a body length away, she stopped and locked eyes with the dark merrow. Familiar black eyes in a sneering pale face stared back at her.

Shree spoke first. "So, have you come all this way to gloat?"

Kira was taken aback. "No, not at all. I'm not that kind of merrow."

"Of course not!" Shree snapped. "You are the virtuous one. You've come to show mercy and kindness to your defeated prisoners?"

Kira shook her head. What was Shree talking about? Then it became clear. Shree did not know that Kira was also a prisoner.

"Why would I want to imprison you? We just wanted you out of our palace."

"Do not be coy with me, merrowling. You put my own nephew up to this trickery, this betrayal—he and his Spegar allies." Shree rose from the bottom and stretched out to her full length. She was longer than Kira. Her tail fin appeared to be shredded but was, in fact, serrated like a bread knife.

Kira felt herself backing away slightly. "Your nephew?" she said.

Shree laughed and raked the water with her clawed hands, as if tearing down a curtain between them. "Ha! You did not know Jarmu was my nephew? You merrows are such guileless creatures, especially you, little princess." If they had been on land, Kira was certain Shree would have been spitting at her.

"He is handsome as far as merrows are concerned," she continued. "My sister Krona chose his merrow father carefully. I am certain Jarmu has you twisted into love knots, you silly merrowling."

"I have no idea what or who you are talking about!"

Shree waved her clawed hands as if she were shooing away a bothersome eel. "You know him. He uses many names—Jens, Janus, James—whatever suits his purposes. Fair and handsome, he is a perfect merrow or human on the outside. But inside, he roils and burns like his mother, my dear expired sister. Oh my, you look surprised." She grinned, flashing her pointed teeth.

Kira remained silent. Was Shree telling the truth or trying to confuse her?

Shree's expression darkened with a sudden scowl. "And what has he told you about his plans for this institute of his? If you believe anything he says, you are a fool. I want to know why I am here. I demand to be released at once!"

Shree lunged at Kira, morphing into a fully spiked finfolk as she struck out. Kira was ready for her, easily dodging the claws and streaking over and behind Shree toward Henry. He held the gun in his outstretched hand and pointed it directly at Shree.

Within seconds, Kira had jumped out and stood dripping on the deck. She peered anxiously into the water. Had Henry fired a shot? He emerged at the opposite side from her, joining Cody at that end of the pool.

"Everyone okay?" Sarah called out. "Wally, did you get that?"

Kira looked over to Wally, who had been filming the encounter. "Yeah, what I could in this lighting. That was amazing! What is that thing?"

Shree remained in her finfolk skin, lying still as a burnt black log at the bottom of the pool.

Henry had returned his gun to the holster. He spoke quietly to Sarah and Cody. Kira saw them nodding their heads.

Kira looked back down at Shree. There was no movement. Was she playing stunned or dead? Had Henry shot her? Kira couldn't believe that they didn't seem more concerned.

"Shouldn't we check to see if she's okay?" she called out.

"No!" Sarah and Henry shouted together.

"She's dangerous," he said. "Probably just stunned. She'll be fine."

They all left and returned to Kira's garden. Before she could slip back into the water, Sarah stopped her. She wanted to know whether that was a merrow or some other creature, and, of course, she was curious about what they had said to each other.

"No, that was a finfolk. They can change into different forms underwater when they wish to, but they can't change into humans. They're hideous on land." Kira sighed. She thought carefully about her next words. "This one was angry at being captured. She wanted to know why she was here, and she demanded to be released—immediately. Then she came at me."

Sarah frowned. "You never told me about finfolk." Her tone suggested that Kira had let her down.

"Well, I'm sorry. You never asked," Kira said, exasperated. "They're nasty, dangerous creatures, and that was really upsetting. If you don't mind, I think I'll go back to my room now!" She dove in, exhilarated at her mini tantrum. Sometimes it was difficult to remember that she wasn't a human; she had only been raised as one.

Kira swam full circuits and then figure eights around the pool for a long time before she settled to the bottom, exhausted. She hadn't lied to Sarah—she really was upset. Janus, merrow of many names, was Shree's nephew? Really? She didn't want to believe Shree, but why would she lie to Kira?

It actually made some sense. Shree knew about the Spegars. Janus may have invited them to come if he had a plan to take over Merhaven with their help. They were so keen to see the palace that day she was captured by them, and they specifically wanted her. Was Janus going to ransom her? What was his plan? Why had he disappeared without a trace and never contacted the others after the attack?

And how had Shree been transported to the institute without someone seeing her in that ugly reptilian form? Had they kept her in water the entire time? Why didn't anyone know what she really was? Or did they know and just wanted to see what would happen when Kira interacted with a finfolk in merrow form?

Kira couldn't wait to talk to Cody again and tell him what she'd learned from Shree. Maybe he could check into Janus and find out whether he was, in fact, associated with the institute.

A buzz interrupted her musings, so Kira rose to the surface to see who was visiting this late in the day. Cody stood on the deck in his diving suit, holding two helmets. Kira wanted to shout, "Have you been reading my mind? Get in here!" However, she managed to keep her lips clamped shut.

"Coralene, sorry to be here so late. I just thought this would be a good opportunity to take a few measurements. I assume you've been swimming hard to ease the tension?" Cody squatted at the edge of the deck and handed her a helmet.

Kira jumped into the spirit of the invitation and accepted the headgear. "Yes, Dr. Morton. You want to measure an exhausted mermaid? Why not?"

Cody nodded his head in agreement, turned on the monitors, and then slipped into the pool. Kira had already attached her helmet— she'd become proficient at this routine. After swimming a few feet from the deck underwater, they both gave big sighs and laughed.

"It was Shree, wasn't it?" Cody began.

Kira spilled the details of the entire conversation in under a minute.

"So, you think she was telling the truth?" Cody asked.

"I don't know, but it's possible. Or perhaps she wanted to turn me against Janus. Can you find out if he's involved with IMMI? See if anyone is named James something."

"Sure. I have a list of the directors, the staff, and some of the investors. They even have photos of the bigwigs on their boardroom wall. We dug up a lot of information on this group. They're definitely out for profit, not science." Cody paused and then cleared his throat, signalling more to come.

"I should tell you, Kira, that Shree didn't survive being shot with Henry's stun gun."

"Oh" was all she could say. She had hoped to talk to Shree again, if her nemesis ever calmed down, and find out more about this place and Janus's involvement. She was not exactly sad that Shree had died, but she was disappointed, nonetheless.

"And there's something else," Cody continued. "They took me down to their necropsy suite so I could have a look at Shree. They were already starting to cut her open, to study her organs."

Kira could feel her stomach beginning to flutter.

"But even worse, there were other bodies. Most were covered, but I think I saw the fins of a merrow."

"Oh no! Not Maya?"

"I don't think so, not the bit I saw. It was plain grey and thicker, not the filmy colours of Maya's tail fin. Of course, I didn't see the other bodies—"

"Cody, we've got to get out of here. Soon!"

Cody grabbed Kira's hands and squeezed them.

"We will, I promise. I've already submitted my request for testing at Sea Lion Cove, and it's been approved by the study protocol office. We need one more signature, and then we can go."

"Whose?"

"One of the directors, but I don't know which one. I think it's just a formality, though. Anyway, the entire place is enclosed by fencing, right across the ocean inlet. The fences are anchored into the rocks underwater and extend four feet above the water at high tide and up to ten feet at low tide. Plus, they use the same force field they have in here, in case the fence isn't enough to keep people and animals out."

"Or keep them inside. Will it be turned on while we're doing the tests?"

"No, fortunately. That would interfere with my sensors and recording equipment. We turn the shield off here as well when I'm working with you. We're assuming you won't make a run for it, of course." Cody grinned at her through his glass faceplate.

"Of course," Kira said, smiling back.

"So, Kira, how high did you say you could jump?"

"High enough, Cody. I'll make it over that fence at low tide for sure. What about you? How will you get out if you're inside the cove with me?"

"Well, I've eliminated blasting through the fence or pre-cutting a hole as possible escape routes since they check the fence routinely. I wouldn't count on walking or driving out the way we came in, either, because they might be a little suspicious by then." He paused.

"You're not planning to climb out, are you?"

"Actually, I am. I'll ditch the flippers and climb."

Kira was shaking her head.

"I'm very good at it, Kira. I did a lot of climbing up and down on that research vessel. It's only a few feet."

"Really?" She was not convinced. "What if they shoot at you?"

"Except for Henry's stun gun, I haven't seen anyone packing firearms."

"Yeah, but they probably don't need them here, on the inside. I can't break out, and I'm no threat to anyone. I don't know about this. Climbing out sounds too risky."

"Low risk, I assure you. Anyway, you're worth it. I'm not leaving this place without you, Kira."

Kira stared at Cody, her mouth agape. She tore off her helmet and threw her arms around him, the way she'd wanted to when he'd first revealed his identity. He hugged her back tightly, and they clung to each other for a long while. Kira had that tingly sensation of being held by an emotional merrow, except this contact felt warm and soothing and she did not want to let go. Ever. When they finally unclasped, Kira laughed and pointed to the tears floating away from her eyes. Cody smiled, but his eyes were also wet behind the glass. She kissed her palm and then placed it on the glass over his lips. Her heart beat wildly when she realized she wanted to feel his lips on hers.

Cody's mouth formed the word "wow," and then he grinned. They held hands as they returned to the edge of the pool. Cody climbed out, removed his helmet, and turned off the monitors. Kira unclipped the sensors and handed them back to him.

"Thank you, Coralene, for being so cooperative. I hope we'll be able to replicate some of these measurements in the larger outdoor facility soon. Real fieldwork, none of this laboratory stuff, eh?"

"I agree, Dr. Morton. Have a good evening."

"Sweet dreams," he whispered, winking at her as he turned for the door.

Kira drifted to the bottom, sobbing. A new awareness had taken hold—she was terrified by the risk Cody was taking to set her free, more afraid than of any harm that might come to her.

Chapter 18 –
Sea Lion Cove

KIRA'S DREAMS were anything but sweet. She woke several times through the night to banish disturbing images—cut up pieces of merrows floating past her or finfolk who had died and come back to life to hunt her down. She had never been a fan of zombie stories, not like her classmates who devoured everything they could read or watch on these morbid, fantastical creatures. Once Kira learned of her true nature and of the existence of other supposedly mythical beings, she began to worry that vampires and zombies might also be as real as merrows. Other times she wondered if she'd been living a troubling dream all her life. If so, when would she ever wake up?

Sarah was the person who greeted her the next morning. Her puppeteer, as Kira had begun to think of her. Kira, dull and groggy from her rough night, was disappointed it was not Cody on the deck.

"Good morning, Coralene," Sarah said, but not with her usual cheeriness. "Dr. Morton tells me you were pretty upset with what happened, and I don't blame you. We shouldn't have put you in the pool with that monster. I'm really sorry."

Kira nodded. "None of us knew what she really was. They're tricky creatures." She felt a prickle of irritation, growing into something stronger. What if Sarah *had* known what she was doing all along? "So, when they brought her here, what form was she in?" Kira asked. "Finfolk can't take a human form on land, you know."

Sarah's face went blank for a moment, and then she furrowed her brow. "Uh, I don't know. I never saw her come in."

"Do you know who brought her? They should have told you about how strange she was. They have four legs on land and long snouts with rows of sharp triangular teeth, like sharks. No one could miss that."

Kira watched Sarah's mouth twitch and pull tight. Kira was certain that Sarah knew who had brought Shree in. However, it was possible she had not been informed about Shree's true identity.

"Well," she began, her back stiffening, "she didn't change her form when they took her out of the water yesterday. She still had the tail and spikes. And yeah, she had a lot of sharp teeth, but not a long snout."

Kira sighed. "Once they're dead, they can't morph anymore."

"Okay, maybe so. Anyway, what I came to tell you is that we got the okay to do some outdoor testing at Sea Lion Cove. Dr. Morton and Wally are out there now to scope it out and set up equipment."

Kira let out her breath and inhaled again before she spoke. "When?"

"Um, tomorrow maybe or the next day. It depends on how long it takes to set things up and on the weather. But it looks like clear skies for the whole week, so that shouldn't hold us up."

"Wow, that's great. Thanks Sarah." Kira did not want to sound too enthusiastic. She couldn't tell Sarah how much she missed the fresh outdoor air and warm sunshine on her skin. That would not be consistent with a merrow who supposedly lived mostly underwater.

Kira spent the rest of the day cruising her pool, eating, and taking frequent short naps. At the first hint of dreaming, she awoke and launched into a vigorous swim. She tried not to think of Shree at all or of Janus being involved in capturing merrows. Unfortunately, it began to make sense that he was the one who had delivered Shree. Under the cover of night, no one would know what kind of beast he had snared.

Kira tried to imagine how he could have pulled it off by himself. He had to have help, maybe from a Spegar or two or from local thugs he had paid off. Perhaps Shree had been transported in a large container of water, though that would have been very heavy and awkward to move. Another possibility is they trussed and wrapped her up so she couldn't escape or hurt anyone or, most importantly, be properly seen. After all, Kira had been moved and delivered at night several times now. This appeared to be the normal operating procedure for smugglers of exotic marine life.

Kira was enormously relieved when Cody showed up late in the evening. She'd had way too much time to think and fret that day, and she craved some reassurance.

"Okay, Miss Coralene," he said, clapping his hands together. "Looks like we got everything ready to go in one day. The equipment is all in place, and it's working well. And you? Are you ready for a field trip?" He couldn't help but grin as he continued to rub his hands together.

Kira nodded her head and continued the deception of innocence. "Yes! Totally! I can't wait to be in natural ocean water again. I know this water is piped in from the coast, but it's not the same, not even with the skylights in here."

"Exactly. And we'll have a much longer straight run for you to test speed and endurance. We'll start with baseline measurements once we get you ready to go with sensors. I think we'll fit you out with the helmet at first so we can repeat our earlier readings, and you and I can communicate underwater in case anything needs to be adjusted. Then we'll repeat the manoeuvres without the helmet, like before."

Kira felt like a bobblehead doll as she listened and nodded. It was really going to happen. She couldn't wait to be out of this fish bowl, where she had to watch what she did or said out of the water.

"So, Coralene, get a good night's sleep if you can. It's late, and we're both tired, so I'll prep you on the order of tests on our drive out there." Cody removed his glasses and raised his eyebrows at Kira. He pretended to clean his lenses and then put the glasses back on.

"Good night, Coralene," he said curtly and nodded before he left.

"Good night, Dr. Morton." She smiled. Cody made an excellent science geek turned spy.

***

KIRA WAS SURPRISED to be awakened by the morning buzzer. She had slept soundly that night, though she hadn't expected to. It had been a dreamless sleep, which was rare for her. She hoped that was a good sign.

Within half an hour, Kira was outside in the warm California air, taking in satisfying deep breaths. Two husky guards escorted her to a long black car and opened a back door for her. Cody was already inside the darkened vehicle, with a laptop computer on the seat beside him. Kira sat on the other side of the laptop.

In the front passenger seat, Sarah turned around as Kira settled in. "So, are you excited about this outing?" she asked.

"Well, yeah, I'm really happy to get outside, and I'm looking forward to being in the ocean again. I've never been in the Pacific before."

"It won't be too different from your garden, you know. You'll see all the same species of fish and plants. The bottom may be a little more natural."

Kira smiled and nodded. Sarah was not the person she wanted to talk to. She was disappointed to see her in their car, for there were other vehicles driving out as well. Besides the technician, Kira knew there would be a security team to keep an eye on her. Some would even be underwater, watching from a distance. They were the ones she worried about when the time came for Cody to do his Spider-Man routine up and over the fence. Another horrible thought had also occurred to her. What if they turned the power on and electrocuted him before he got over?

Cody cleared his throat. "So, Coralene, here is the order of tests we're going to begin with. These should be familiar to you by now."

He clicked on the screen, and Kira saw the names of the tests and approximate times next to them. She nodded as he clicked on each one and reviewed them with her. The tests were scheduled so the tide would be at its highest point near the end, conveniently coinciding with her break for the open ocean.

"I thought we'd have a brief pause here after that last swim, after you remove your helmet and before you repeat the series."

He looked at Kira and raised his eyebrows. She felt herself tense as she gave a slight nod. He clicked on a small icon in the corner of the screen, and a photo popped into view. It was of a young man dressed in a suit and tie. His confident smile contrasted sharply with the emptiness of his cold dark eyes. To Kira, this was the most sinister expression she'd ever seen on Janus's face. Beneath the photo was written the name "Mr. James Falconshire." Then, with a quick tap of Cody's finger, the photo disappeared.

"Sure, that looks fine to me." She nodded at Cody. "I'm looking forward to the exercise, but I'll probably want a little break by then."

Twenty minutes later, they arrived at the cove. As Cody had explained, they entered through a secure gate in a high chain-link fence. The car stopped in a parking lot next to a small brick building. Two other cars were already there, and three men, including Henry, were pulling on their wetsuits.

"Dr. Morton," Sarah said, "since you won't be needing me here, I'll head down to the nearby marina. I thought I'd go for a boat ride and see some of the local area. I haven't had a chance to do that yet."

"Will you go back from there or come back here first?" Cody asked her.

"Wally will call me when you're nearly done, and I'll meet you here for the ride back to the institute." Sarah was all smiles and waved at them before getting back into the car.

Cody raised his eyebrows again at Kira. "It is a lovely day for a boat ride," he said quietly. "I wonder if we'll see them on the other side of the barrier, cruising by on their scenic tour."

Kira shrugged, but she was worried. Now there was another layer of security on the outside of the fence. Her keepers were leaving nothing to chance. They might even spot the vessel that was waiting for Kira and Cody around the north point and farther out at sea.

The security divers were underwater by the time Cody had suited up, and they both had their helmets on. Kira was delighted by the sensation of waves lapping at her feet and legs as she waded in. She squinted at the clear azure sky and the sun warming her face, pausing a moment to soak it up. This could be the last time she would ever do this if their plan failed. No, she had to be positive. This was going to be her first day of freedom in months.

Kira dove in and swam forward, enjoying the sight of plants anchored in real earth and sand, of fish freely swimming next to her, of the massaging tug and push of the waves on her scaly merrow body. This was freedom: moving unhindered in the cove, knowing she could outswim any of the guards in that encircled space.

"Coralene. Where are you?" Cody's voice rang inside her helmet. "Enjoying your swim?"

Kira laughed. "As a matter of fact, I am. I'm doing a warm-up right now."

"Okay, mermaid-on-turbo-boosters. Let's save that for the tests. You'll need to reserve some energy. We have a lot of runs to make today."

Kira giggled. "Oh yeah, I almost forgot. I'm high on seawater,

I guess."

"Swim up to where Wally's sitting with the monitors. We'll show him our nice round helmet heads and wave. I need to make sure the sensors are working anyway."

"Yes sir, on my way, sir!"

Kira popped up first and startled Wally only a few feet away, perched on a rock ledge above her. She waved at him, and he waved back. A moment later, Cody's head emerged. He and Wally spoke through their headphones, leaving Kira out of the conversation. Finally, Cody addressed her.

"We're good to go. Now we'll have you swim to the yellow marker along the rocks on this side. Let me know when you get there. Then wait until I give you the signal to swim across to the yellow marker on the other side of the cove."

"Got it, boss."

"And all things considered, let's forgo the high-speed return run. Tell me when you arrive on the other side. At that point, remove the sensors and the helmet. Remember how to secure it. Then go into overdrive to the target. I'm on my way now. Good luck."

Kira's heart began to hammer as she swam to the large yellow stripe. Cody was on his way to the fence, where he would wait for her jump. This was much sooner than they had planned, but then again, they hadn't known Sarah would be patrolling on the other side of the barrier. That was a complication they didn't need.

"Okay, I'm here now," Kira said. "Finger on the button, ready to launch across."

"Go!" Cody said.

Kira pushed the button signalling her push away from the marker to begin a moderately fast swim across the cove. She wondered if her racing heart might alert Wally that something wasn't right, but she couldn't calm down knowing what was ahead. Anyway, she reasoned with herself, Wally wasn't there to analyze the data, just to make sure the monitors were working and the sensors' information was being recorded.

The cove was three quarters of a mile across, about 1.2 kilometres, she'd been told. She really wanted to pop up to see how close she was, but she was not allowed to do so for the test. It seemed to be taking forever, but she kept a steady speed as instructed, since that would also be recorded.

Finally, the dark, rocky south side of the cove loomed ahead. Kira noticed a movement on her left that seemed out of place—one of the security divers. He waved at her as she passed by. Kira stared at him, her heart about to explode, but then gave him a small wave in return. He remained where he was as she continued to her marker on the rocks, her heart still racing.

When she finally reached the rock face and looked up to make sure she was at the yellow stripe, she pushed the button again, signalling her arrival. Kira remained underwater and looked left and right to see if any of the other guards were nearby. She saw no one. The guard she had passed by must have remained where he was, or he had swum elsewhere.

Kira dove to the bottom to search for loose rocks. There were none in her immediate area, and she began to panic. She swam west, in the direction of the fence, hugging the coast until she finally spotted several rocks in the sandy bottom. She tugged until one of the rocks loosened. It felt heavy enough.

"Dr. Morton, I'm almost ready to do the return lap."

"Very good, Coralene." Cody's voice was calm. It soothed her like a puppy being caressed by a loving owner.

"Okay, preparing to launch."

With those words, Kira detached the helmet, ripped off the sensors, and stuffed them inside the helmet along with the rock so it would not float up. She then placed them on the bottom. She scooped some nearby sand over the helmet for good measure and then launched herself toward freedom.

At some point during her swim for the fence, Kira knew she'd have to get close to the surface to determine the distance for her jump. She'd only seen it from the shore, which was nearly a mile away. The tide was still coming in, so the fence would be on the high side, at least six to eight feet and possibly even ten feet or more, depending on erratic surges. The spot she chose to make her jump was important. The depth at that takeoff spot was also critical for reaching the speed she needed to clear the fence.

Why had she told Cody she could do this? In the Panamanian aquarium, she'd had lots of time to practice, and she'd known the heights involved. Here she was in the dark, making guesses and improvising as she went along. Cody's life was at stake, not just hers. Kira realized then that she had to make the jump no matter what and that she probably had only one chance to do so.

Sensing the fence was not far off, Kira neared the surface to have a quick look. She did not have to break through to the air—she could see the fence through the top layer of water. She dove to the bottom and swam up to the fence more slowly. From there, she could gauge the depth of the water. It was going to be barely enough to get the speed she'd need. She would have to back up farther to gain the required momentum.

She turned around and began to swim away from the fence, concentrating on the ground marks and how far she was going. She almost missed the movement off to her right, closer to the side from which she had just come. Kira sank into a clump of seagrass behind a small rock outcropping. She watched as one of the divers slowly passed by, fortunately heading away from the fence. When he had been gone for a few minutes, she continued her swim for a few more body lengths, skirting the bottom.

Then Kira turned around. She remained still for a moment, gathering her focus and willing her muscles to obey. She pushed off, beating hard with her tail, streamlined, with her hands making a V-shape that sliced through the water. At first, she hugged the bottom; then she began to angle upward, beating harder. As she approached, she could feel the resistance of water through the heavy fencing and she pushed with all the strength in her body.

Kira thought of all the mean, hateful people who imprisoned, tortured, and killed innocent merrows and dolphins, and she found herself screaming as she burst through the surface and became a flying missile. She shot into the air, up and up, along the fence, her body slowing until she could make out each wire diamond reflecting the sun. She wasn't going to make it!

"No!" she screamed again as the fence evaporated into clear sky and water ahead. She was at the top! Kira curved her body and flipped her tail as high as she could. For a moment she hovered, barely moving, until she saw the water directly below her on the other side. She felt a searing pain as her tail scraped across the top edge of the jagged fence, but she was on her way down now, plummeting too fast to look for Cody. She only had time to scan the ocean horizon for boats as she reached the water. She saw none.

I made it, I made it, she thought, slicing through the surface of the free Pacific Ocean on the other side. She swam a few feet away and then resurfaced, searching the fence for any sign of Cody climbing over. She saw nothing, heard nothing but the sound of the moving water and waves crashing on the rocky coastline on either side of her.

Kira swam toward the northern shore, thinking that Cody was closer to that side when she'd left him earlier.

Finally, she heard a shout in the distance. Squinting, she managed to make out someone climbing over the fence, near the top. Kira dove underwater and raced to the spot. She felt drained yet energized by her jump and near miss. She was desperate to get to Cody before anyone else could. As she surfaced again, she heard a loud yell and witnessed the climber at the top of the fence tumbling into the water on her side.

Kira arrived as Cody was sinking. The fact that he was making no attempt to swim or even move his limbs alarmed her. She grabbed him and looked into his faceplate. His eyes were closed; his mouth, slack.

No, she thought. Had he been electrocuted? No! This couldn't be. She'd made it over, and so had he. He had to be okay!

Kira put her arms under his and hugged him close to her. She beat her tail hard to get as far from the fence as she could. Her pace was sluggish with the extra weight. Her tail ached as though it had been crushed in a rock avalanche. She looked back to see a trail of her blood behind her.

Kira was determined to get to the rendezvous. They had gone too far to stop now. She cried as she limped along with her precious cargo, all the while urging Cody to wake up. She was sure his heart was still beating. Or was it her own, throbbing from the exertion?

Kira swam into a small depression in the rocky coast and dragged Cody down to rest on a patch of sand. She was still crying. Kira placed her hand over Cody's heart.

"Beat, damn it, beat!" She could feel nothing. "No!" She grabbed Cody and held him tightly, her chest pounding against his still one. She sobbed and gripped him harder. Then she felt a tingling heat in her chest, growing until it felt like a fire. Was she having a heart attack?

It didn't matter. She would not let go of Cody. If he were dead, she would die down here with him.

Suddenly Kira was jerked up and away from Cody. He was sitting up; his eyes and mouth were wide open. He raised his arm and pointed at her.

This had to be a nightmare. Was Cody in his death throes? Had he turned into a zombie? Not that, no!

He was talking. He was mouthing her name, still pointing. Kira put her hands on her thudding chest, now only warm. She looked down and saw her Pendright glowing brightly. She looked up at Cody, grinning at her. He was no zombie. He was alive!

She rushed back and threw her arms around him. He embraced her in return. Kira put her hand over his heart—a loud, lively beating heart. She started to cry again, heaving with sobs. Cody patted her back and then rubbed her arms. When they broke apart, he pointed to her injured tail. It had mostly stopped bleeding but was still sore. He pointed away and motioned for them to leave. He then glanced at her tail and raised his hands, palms up, as if asking a question.

"I'll be okay," she mouthed to assure him. She then beat her tail to show that it still worked. She clamped her lips tight against the pain.

As they started off, Kira wondered how far they would get with her injury and with Cody's recent revival from the brink of death. Without his flippers, he led the way slowly, around the rocky promontory and away from the cove. Somewhere, hopefully not too far away, Borin should be waiting for them. Kira realized with a sinking heart that Borin was not only her cousin but also Janus's. If Shree had told the truth, then Borin could be part of the bigger plan. Had Borin known Janus's real identity all along? Were they about to fall into a trap?

Chapter 19 –
Finding Home

KIRA LOOKED AT CODY and tried to push her doubts aside. He was so eager, so hopeful as they struggled against the current, trying to avoid the crashing surf and jagged volcanic rocks. However, the nagging thoughts wouldn't leave her. If they discovered Borin alone, could they overpower him if they had to? If it were a trap, she assumed he'd have help. Without weapons and weakened by their escape efforts, they were easy pickings for any enemy they came across, including large sharks.

Just as she had that thought, Kira and Cody both noticed several dark shapes in the deeper water on their left. Before Kira could react, the fuzzy forms resolved into giant orange-brown turtles, a bale of fifteen to twenty of them. They paddled at a leisurely pace, though still faster than Kira and Cody could swim. He pointed at the turtles and Kira nodded—they would hitch a ride with the easygoing giants.

Within seconds, they had hooked onto the forward carapace edges of the two largest turtles. Loggerhead sea turtles, with their bright-yellow-edged shells, were not often seen along the California coast. Kira imagined how thrilled Cody must be. She tried to speak to the turtles, and though a couple turned their beaked heads her way, they did not respond. She laughed at their placid expressions, wishing she could feel as calm and carefree as they appeared. One of the smaller turtles looked at her and made a gurgling noise that sounded like laughter. Turtle gurgles. Kira laughed louder, and several other turtles responded with gurgles. Up ahead of her, Cody did not seem to notice—he couldn't hear the sounds through his helmet. She'd have to tell him about this later.

Eventually the turtles surfaced to breathe, and after looking at the coastline, Cody motioned to Kira that they had arrived at the right spot. They let go of their turtle mounts, and Kira laughed a goodbye. The turtles gurgled and moved on without breaking stride. They were migrating, probably to a specific location to mate or to lay eggs. Kira hoped they would have a safe journey in spite of all the dangers and obstacles in their way—fishing nets that could entangle and drown them, as well as plastic garbage they often mistook for their favourite food, jellyfish. Fortunately, hunting giant sea turtles was illegal in most countries, and their populations were slowly recovering from past slaughters.

Kira looked at Cody to see what he wanted to do. He mimed with his hands around his mouth. He wanted her to call out. He mouthed a word. Apparently, he wanted to play underwater charades. He held up one finger, indicating the first syllable: "Oh," Kira guessed. He then held up two fingers for the second syllable, but it seemed undecipherable to Kira. Was the syllable "it," "in," or "win"? She tried both syllables together: "Oh-win." Kira shrugged, thinking it made no sense. They were here to rendezvous with Borin. Of course, the mystery word was "Bo-rin"! Did she really want to call her cousin, who may or may not be an ally of theirs? Would they be able to find the rescue ship without him, as disabled as they were?

Kira closed her eyes briefly and pictured the scene on the boat after reclaiming Merhaven—she and Borin crying as they embraced and shared their grief. He was her family.

"Borin!" she shouted. Their proximity to the coast meant that the water was murky with wave-stirred sand, so she could not see far into the distance. That made her nervous. They had no weapons, nothing to protect themselves. She looked at Cody next to her and noticed for the first time that he had a sheath strapped to his right leg. She pointed to it.

Cody grinned, unsnapped the top, and withdrew a long, narrow knife. He brandished it in front of him like a sword and then sheathed the weapon again. Kira clapped her hands in relief. The two of them settled on the sand and waited. After a few minutes, Cody motioned to her to try calling again. She did.

Suddenly a figure appeared from the north, swimming straight at them. Kira froze, but Cody waved his arms in greeting. She wished he had his knife sheath unsnapped, but Cody was oblivious to her state of mind. As Borin approached them, she saw that he had something long strapped to his back. However, she couldn't make out what it was.

"Kira!" he greeted with a broad smile. For a moment, she thought he might hug her, but he stopped short, shaking hands with Cody instead.

Kira swallowed before she spoke. "We're so glad to see you. Is the ship very far? Cody can't swim fast without his flippers, and I'm not so speedy myself." She pointed to her tail. "Attacked by a fence. But I won."

"Looks bad," Borin said, shaking his head. "We've got a bit of a swim and should move out right away. There's a small boat up top, looking for you two I'd guess. I don't know if they have divers, but we've got to get out of here."

Kira nodded. "Yeah, I believe at least one of them is from the institute. And we don't want to bump into them."

Borin twisted around, and Kira finally saw the speargun on his back. "Let's go," he said. "Can you swim faster than this useless human?"

Kira stared at him, annoyed with his brash, insulting attitude. He was laughing, however, with his hand resting companionably on Cody's back. This wasn't the Borin she was used to.

"If we each take him under one arm, we can make better time," he suggested.

"Sure," Kira agreed.

They scooped Cody up and began their final leg to freedom. They had not gone far when Kira heard the rumble of an engine above them. The water here was relatively shallow, so they could not dive deeper to escape detection. Human eyes should not be able to see them, Kira thought, unless the hunters had equipment like sonar to sweep the water below the boat.

"Keep swimming," Borin said quietly.

The stabbing pain in Kira's lower body grew sharper the harder she beat her tail. She gritted her teeth and kept going. She was not going to be captured again, ever.

Kira glanced up at the boat. It had slowed but seemed to be keeping pace just behind them. Then she saw the figure below the boat. It was a diver holding what looked like a small cannon.

"Borin! Look up. They're going to shoot at us!"

"Faster!" he urged.

"I can't, Borin! Take out the speargun. We can't let them take us. We have to fight!"

While Kira clung to Cody, who had finally seen the diver, Borin unsnapped the holster and began to swing the speargun into his hands. Cody unsheathed his knife. The three of them faced the diver, who was approaching them at great speed.

"It's a merrow!" Kira shouted.

Borin growled. "Or finfolk." He lifted the gun to his shoulder and took aim.

Before Borin could pull the trigger, the diver shot his cannon. They lost sight of him in a cloud of bubbles. Suddenly they were crushed together in a jam of legs and arms.

"No!" Kira screamed. They were wrapped in her worst nightmare, a net—and not just any net, but a sticky finfolk net like the one she had run into in the waters of Hildaland. "No, it can't be, not again," she moaned.

The merrow-shaped diver approached, grinning and showing off his normal merrow teeth. Janus.

"Greetings, Kira. So nice to see you again. And with friends. You will not escape again. You have cost me too much already—not after the Spegars lied and stole you from me. What humans call a double-cross, I believe."

He laughed and turned away. Gripping the cannon, he swam slowly back up to the boat. The attached net dragged behind him, like a spider hauling in its trapped prey.

Borin's growling had grown louder. He was struggling and poking Kira with his elbows as he shifted next to her.

"It's no use, Borin," Kira said. "We need Cody's knife to cut ourselves out of this net." She tried to turn her head toward Cody, but his back was to her. She couldn't see his arms or where the knife was.

Borin grunted. "No time for that. All I need is one shot. I had it. I should have pulled the trigger. Just move over, Kira. Yes, there. Sorry."

Kira was furious. Janus was indeed the most hateful finfolk monster of them all, worse than even Shree. This time, Shree had not lied to her.

Borin had stopped squirming. "Don't move, Kira," he said, his voice low and calm. "Here goes."

She felt the discharge of the speargun vibrate through Borin's body.

"Got him!" Borin yelled.

Kira turned her head. Janus had dropped the cannon and was writhing in the water. Blood poured from a wound in the mid-tail, like what had happened to Elder Crane in the Spegar attack. Would Janus die like their old merrow friend? Kira felt her heart go cold and black as she pictured Janus lying dead on the seabed, his body ravaged by a shiver of sharks.

Her thoughts turned into reality before her eyes. As the cannon hit the bottom and the three of them settled gently onto the sand like a deflated balloon, the sharks began to appear. They circled Janus, who continued to flail and sink. Then a strange transformation took place before their eyes, one that amazed and disgusted Kira. Beside her, Borin shook as Janus's features darkened, elongated, and sharpened into the form of their true enemy, a finfolk.

"What in the name of Neptune is that?" he asked. "It's not possible, is it?"

Kira could not speak for a moment. She watched as the sharks finally began their voracious attack, shredding the hybrid of merrow and finfolk into bite-sized pieces until the water whirled into a bloody storm.

Should she tell Borin? No, she didn't need to. It was obvious that Janus had been at least half finfolk. Borin didn't need to know he was related to that monster—if, in fact, that part happened to be true. No, she would not repeat what she'd been told by a conniving, evil finfolk who once pretended to be queen.

"Borin," she finally spoke, "this is bad. Will the sharks come for us? I don't know how much air Cody has left. We've been down here too long. We're stuck, unless Cody can get his knife out." Kira poked Cody with her elbow, and he poked her back.

"He's still alive," she reported, greatly relieved.

Borin fidgeted. "I don't have anything sharp," he said. "I'll see if I can get that knife from Cody."

Kira could feel Borin trying to move his arm. At the same time,

Cody was trying to move his legs.

"Cody took his knife out before we were shot. He might not be able to move it without getting cut. It was really sharp and long. We don't need any more bloodshed with those sharks so close."

"I know, I know. Any other ideas?"

At that moment, they noticed the sharks had begun to race away from their feast, most of them disappearing in the same direction.

"Uh-oh. Maybe a rescue coming for Janus?" Kira said.

"I can't see anything yet. Wait. What's that above us?"

The water suddenly darkened, as if a huge thunderhead had suffocated the sun.

"This is big, big trouble, Kira. We're about to be swallowed whole!"

Kira looked around frantically. "What?"

They were rushing to the surface, as though on a high-speed elevator. They then burst into the air where the sun was still shining in a clear blue sky. The crane that had lifted them out was a large dark-red tentacle. And like a submarine surfacing, a round red dome emerged from the water next to them. An enormous eye ogled them as they swung in the air.

"Borin! We're not going to be eaten. We've just been rescued by one of my friends or a relative of his. I can't tell them apart."

Borin smacked the side of his speargun. "Neptune has been good to us. My message got through."

Just as suddenly as they had been lifted, they were submerged again, and they found themselves rushing through the water, tucked under the giant eight-armed beast of the deep sea. Within minutes they rose out of the water again, this time alongside a ship. The arm holding their net suspended them over the deck and slowly lowered them. They landed with a thump, and then the arm detached and slid back into the water.

Moments later, they were cut free from the sticky mesh by three crew members. Cody ripped off his helmet and took several deep breaths.

"Oh man, what a ride!" he gasped. He flicked the empty gas canister on his helmet. "Just made it," he said, grinning.

"That's a nasty gash on your leg, young lady." An older woman with short greying hair was kneeling next to Kira and examining her wound. "I'm Katie, by the way. Let's get you down to the first aid station right away. Can you walk?"

Borin and Katie helped Kira stand. She tried not to wince but couldn't help herself. Cody jumped to his feet and then nearly fell over. A sturdy red-haired young woman moved in to steady him.

"Wait!" Kira said. "Cody was electrocuted back there. He needs to be checked out."

"I'm fine," he protested, still leaning against the girl who had her arm around his waist.

"No, you're not! First fried and then nearly asphyxiated. And his heart stopped!" Kira choked, tears burning the back of her eyes. This was too much. Katie urged her forward, and Kira gladly moved, with Borin supporting her on the other side.

Once inside the first aid station, a small room near the galley, Katie helped Kira out of her blue coveralls. Kira stifled a yelp as the outfit was peeled off her bloody leg.

"Okay, looks clean, but it's deep," Katie said. "I'll need to apply some disinfectant before it's stitched up. Let me give you something for the pain. You won't feel the stitching. I have a topical freeze for that."

"I don't need any meds," Kira said, gritting her teeth. She gripped the arm of her chair as Katie rinsed out the wound with a liquid that burned like a blowtorch. Kira grabbed her Pendright with her other hand, and the pain was gone, like ice water dousing a fire. She let out the breath she'd been holding in.

Katie glanced at the glowing metal under Kira's hand. "I'd say that is more than a lucky charm," she said.

Kira nodded. "It's saved me a few times. Are you a doctor?" She watched Katie freeze the skin around her wound with a cooling spray.

"I was a medic in the Royal Canadian Navy before I went back to school for a PhD in marine sciences," she said. "I'm one of Cody and Marina's professors. He probably didn't get a chance to tell you about us and our covert operation." She grinned at Kira's surprised expression.

"No, we had to be careful about what we said and how long we spent talking underwater. He left out a few details."

"Yeah, we know. He reported to us when he could, though it was risky. He had to leave the building to do that, with the hope that his messages wouldn't be intercepted. Technology changes so fast. It's hard to know what the other guys are using, whose stuff is more sophisticated, and so on."

"Marina, is she the girl with the curly red hair?" Kira asked. She had wondered how well the young woman and Cody knew each other. The girl had seemed so concerned about him, so close to him. Kira felt her stomach contort. His relationship with this fellow student made her feel uneasy. They were probably just good friends. Marina had joined him on a secret mission, after all, with high adventure and fun thrown in. She was just a friend helping a friend, right?

"Yes, that's Marina. Bright girl. And Cody is brilliant, as you know."

Katie was nearly done stitching, and Kira had felt nothing as the bloody needle wove in and out of her skin.

"Marina is a great name for someone studying marine biology," Kira said. Then she pictured her mother, Bess, with her wild strawberry-blond hair, and Yvette Doyle's crazy red tangles. Marina had the same hair, the same big eyes, the same big hands.

"She's a merrow, isn't she?" Kira gasped.

Katie smiled. "Mm, not quite. She's a rare hybrid, human and merrow. Most merrow-human couples cannot reproduce."

Like my childless adoptive parents, thought Kira.

Katie brought her a change of clothes. They had prepared well for her arrival and treated her like a princess. Katie showed Kira to her cabin and invited her to take a nap before dinner. Kira lay down on her berth and listened to the soothing sounds of the ship engine, chugging back north along the California coastline toward Canada. The last time she was on a ship she'd been a prisoner; now she was the celebrity guest.

She closed her eyes, but all she saw was Cody and Marina latched together. She must be his girlfriend. Why would she have signed on for this trip if they weren't tight, a couple? Kira felt a tear slide down her cheek onto the pillow. Cody, the chubby geek with braces, had transformed into a handsome tall young man who was not only smart but also thoughtful. Why hadn't she noticed? Why hadn't she realized that her strong attachment to him went way beyond friendship? He was bound to find a girl who'd appreciate him and fall in love with him, as she loved him.

Kira stifled a sob. There was nothing she could do about it. She clutched her Pendright and breathed deeply. She could feel her heart racing, stumbling, breaking into pieces. Marina couldn't possibly love Cody more than she did. Kira finally gave in and wept until, exhausted by the sobbing, she fell asleep.

She awakened to the sound of a gong in the distance, followed by a sharp rap on the door.

"Hello?" she croaked.

"Kira? You awake?" It was Cody.

"Uh, yeah. Just a minute." Kira rose and winced as she swung her injured leg off the bed. She hobbled to the small mirror over a tin washbasin. Her eyes were pink and puffy. Ugh, she looked like a sculpin dragged out of the sea. She splashed cold water on her face and then opened the door.

Cody stood there, towering above the top of the doorframe. He hunched over, looking anxious. "How are you feeling? How is your leg?"

"Oh, I'm okay. The leg is a bit sore, but Dr. Katie did a great job patching me up."

"Yeah, she's awesome. She was the one who organized this whole expedition. We are supposedly on a research trip," he laughed. "We pulled it off, Kira! We did it! We got you back!" He put his arms out toward her as if he were holding an invisible box between them. Or was he inviting her in for a hug?

Kira wasn't sure how to respond, so she raised a hand, and they high-fived with a resounding smack.

"Are you hungry? That was the dinner gong. I'm here to fetch you to the table. Unless you don't want to go."

"Uh, sure, I'll go. I'm starting to get my appetite back after all the excitement."

As she exited through the door, Cody bent down slightly to put his arm around her waist.

"I'll be okay, Cody. I can walk," she said, limping forward.

"Okay." His voice suggested that he didn't believe her.

"How are you feeling, Cody?"

"Great! We have you back. That's the best feeling in the world."

Kira smiled. She couldn't help but notice he said "we," not "I."

In the dining area, Katie was seated at one end of a rectangular table. At the other end sat a bearded man wearing a pale-blue uniform shirt with an insignia. The captain, perhaps? Marina sat at his left, and Borin was next to her. Cody helped Kira into a chair on the captain's right side and then he sat next to her. He introduced her to the captain and Marina.

"Is this the full crew?" Kira asked, wondering who was steering the ship.

Captain Wilkins laughed. "No, Martin Dubuc is in charge right now. He's also our mechanic and technical guru. Don't worry, we're in good hands. No one is chasing us, in case you're worried. We're armed anyway, though no one is supposed to know that. Marty served in the military as a sniper, and Borin is a good shot, too, I hear."

Borin laughed. "If you happen to have a spear available, Kira has great aim and a good strong arm," he suggested and grinned at her. The others chuckled. They had all apparently heard the story of her underwater prowess. Kira smiled and lowered her eyes, suddenly feeling shy and exposed.

When Kira looked up again, she met Marina's large blue eyes across the table. She was indeed a beautiful girl. Kira marvelled at how happy Borin looked next to Marina. She'd never seen him so lighthearted and talkative before. In a very short time, he had transformed from a brooding teenager into someone who exuded hope and contentment. It seemed everyone was changing around her. Even she had changed or, at least, was becoming more aware.

During the dinner, Kira was asked to share her experiences at the institute. Everyone was respectful and waited patiently for her to finish before asking for more details. She warmed up to the conversation and gave them a good idea of the events that had unfolded from the time they were ambushed by the Spegars until Cody came on the scene. She was happy to let Cody and Borin finish the story. They were both vibrating with impatience to provide their own versions.

"So, Borin," Kira finally asked, "you sent for Sherman? Or one of his brothers?"

Borin glanced at Marina before answering. "Yeah, I called your dolphin friends. Cass came right away, and we hatched a plan. What I didn't know was the timing. I wasn't sure whether Sherman got the message and, if so, whether he'd be there for us, if or when we needed him."

"Thank you, Borin. I owe you my life."

"And I owe you my life, too," Cody said. "Thanks, man."

"I owe my life to *all* of you," Kira said. "Thank you for all the risks you've taken, all your time. And I'm sure it must have cost a fortune—" She burst into tears.

Cody put his arm around her while she covered her face and tried to compose herself. Finally, she sat up straight and smiled. "I think I need to go up top for some fresh air." They all nodded, and Cody helped her out of her chair. He walked with her to the stairs and held her arm while she limped up, one slow step at a time.

"You don't need to come up with me," she said.

"I'm ready for some fresh air, too. Do you mind if I come along? Or would you rather be alone?"

"You can come if you like," she said, not meeting his eyes.

Though it was evening, there was still plenty of light. Only a few wispy clouds dotted the sky. The coast was barely visible to the right, and there were no other vessels in view. Kira gripped the rail and faced north, homeward bound. She welcomed the soothing sea breeze on her skin.

"Cody, do my parents know what happened? I've been worried about them all this time, what they've been going through."

"Well, stop worrying, Kira. Currin was the first to let me know when you were taken. And they all know you're safe now. They've stayed busy. Merrows are rebuilding Merhaven. Once we're farther north and out of tracing range, you can talk to them yourself on our satellite phone. You know, all your parents never lost hope that we'd find you."

Kira teared up and faced away from Cody.

"Kira, are you upset with me?"

She whirled around to face Cody. "No! Why would I be upset? After all you've done for me?"

"I don't know. It just feels like you're disappointed in me. I nearly ruined everything by getting caught on the fence like that. And you got hurt. I should have stuck to the original plan and waited for the tide to be higher." He shook his head and frowned. "And then you had to rescue me. What happened out there anyway?"

"I'm not really sure. You were unconscious. I couldn't feel your heartbeat. I was so scared, Cody. I didn't know what to do. I thought you were dead. Electrocuted." Kira gulped and turned back to face into the wind. She closed her eyes and found herself back underwater, terrified and clinging to Cody.

She heard a slam behind them and looked back. Borin and Marina had stepped out onto the deck. They waved, and, for a moment, she thought they would join her and Cody. Instead, Borin took Marina by the hand, and they began to stroll away toward the stern of the boat. Kira's mouth dropped open.

Cody chuckled. "They make a cute couple, don't they?" he said.

Kira gulped and looked up at her best friend. "Yeah. I had no idea. Borin has changed so much in the last few months."

"Falling in love will do that to a person," he said.

Kira thought her heart would burst out of her chest. She could feel the warmth of the Pendright against her skin, and she knew it was glowing. She touched it with one hand and put her other hand on Cody's chest.

"Your heart stopped, Cody. I thought I'd lost you. I hugged you as hard as I could. I thought I was going to burst into flames underwater. Then you were back!"

Leaning down, Cody wrapped his arms around Kira, and they kissed. She thought the Pendright would melt down, but it only pulsed, matching their two hearts, beat for beat.

Cody straightened up and rested his cheek on top of Kira's head. She leaned into his chest, and they hung on to each other for a few minutes more. When they broke apart, they continued to hold hands, staring into each other's eyes.

"I'd do it all again, you know," Cody said. "But this time I'd wait for a higher tide."

Kira laughed. "I shouldn't have led you on, bragging about how high I could jump."

"Seriously, Kira, have you decided where you're going this fall? BC or Newfoundland? Time is running out for registration. It's August twenty-first already."

Dear Cody, so practical, so grounded. Kira cocked her head and furrowed her brow. "I love the program at Memorial, and it's much closer to home. I think my parents would be heartbroken if I went to BC. What do you think?"

Cody shook his head. "I think the program at UBC is superior. And anyway, the climate is more suitable for marine botany study than the northern Atlantic."

"That's it?"

"No, I'm just getting started. My parents have survived my being out here, and yours will, too. They want you to be happy. You'll be happier here, trust me."

"Really?"

"Really. You like to make the people you love happy, right?"

Kira nodded. "Sure."

"So make me happy. Come to UBC with me. Come home."

Kira burst into laughter and threw her arms around Cody's neck. "I am so ready to come home! And now I know where it is."

They kissed again and, a moment later, broke apart to the sounds of clapping, whistling, and cheering from Borin and Marina. Kira knew her face had to be beet red as she stood next to Cody, his arm around her shoulders. Borin, now laughing, threw his arms open, and Kira walked into them to give her cousin a fierce hug. With Cody and Borin nearby, Kira felt more certain than ever about where she belonged and the people who were her family.

The young people talked and joked and laughed together until the dusk deepened to night. When all four yawned simultaneously, they knew it was time for some hard-won sleep. They filed down below deck to their cabins.

Cody stopped at Kira's door. It was deep-sea dark in the narrow hallway, except for a single light farther along the passage.

"Kira," Cody began, "I have a burning question for you before we say goodnight."

"Oh? What is it?"

"Your Pendright. That is one amazing piece of techno-magic. And very pretty, too, I might add. I'd love to figure out how it works. Do you ever take it off?"

"No."

"Oh."

"Not really. It can get shockingly hot."

Cody smiled. "That's okay with me. It's a lifesaver."

"I have a question for you, too."

"Shoot!"

Kira paused, wondering if he meant to use that word as a joke, though he looked serious. "Did you grow the beard for your Dr. Morton disguise? And do you plan to keep it?" She stifled the giggle that was bubbling up.

"Well, here's what happened. It was easier not to shave when we were out at sea and busy all the time. So I just let it grow. When I found out you were missing, and we got some leads on where you might be, the plan fell into place. It was a great disguise. You didn't recognize me!"

"No, but I recognized your voice. I just didn't put it together right away."

"I kind of like the beard. What do you think?"

Kira laughed. "It makes you look a lot older. And it tickles."

"Is that good or bad?"

"I'm not sure. I think I'll need a larger sample size before I decide." The giggle finally burst out.

"More kisses?" Cody asked, his eyes lighting up in the dark hallway.

"Definitely. If we're going to run an experiment, we need to do it right. We're scientists, after all."

"Yes, we are," Cody murmured as he leaned over to kiss Kira goodnight.

Acknowledgements

Writing can be a solitary activity, but it requires a physical and emotional support system. I wish to thank two special people who have always been my champions: Heini, my forever friend, and Kaylan, my niece. And, as ever, I am grateful to the support of my WWW writing group and the vibrant arts community of Prince Edward Island.

I also wish to thank my skilled editors, Penelope Jackson and Hope Digout.